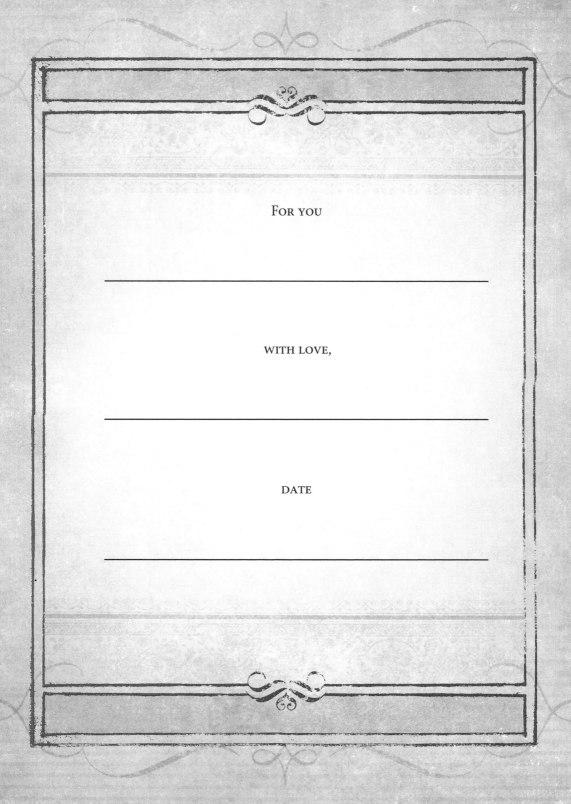

For you

_____

With love,

_____

Date

_____

No person at Howard Books has worked harder than
she where *The Best of Christmas in My Heart* ® collections
are concerned. Being a grandmother many times over, and
firmly committed to Story, both when her children were young
and now with her grandchildren, it has not been a mere abstraction
or something that a job requires of her, to work on these collections,
but rather an opportunity that brings her great joy. A heaven-sent
opportunity to help other grandparents, parents, and extended family
out there who are seeking Christmas stories that are not only
spiritually based but also hold children's interest and inculcate
values worth living by. A black-belted story-buff herself,
she can clearly differentiate between unforgettable
stories and so-so-stories.

She is also a clear-eyed editor, with a sixth sense for introductions:
she strips them down to their very essence, pruning off anything
she considers merely peripheral to the stated purpose.

In short, these two collections would not be what they are
without the enthusiastic involvement of my cherished and
esteemed collaborator. And so it gives me great pleasure to
dedicate *The Best of Christmas in My Heart* ® 2 to:

CHRYS HOWARD

THE BEST OF

Christmas
IN MY
HEART

VOLUME II

COMPILED & EDITED BY
JOE WHEELER

Timeless Stories to Warm Your Heart

HOWARD BOOKS
A DIVISION OF SIMON & SCHUSTER
New York   London   Toronto   Sydney

Our purpose at Howard Books is to:

· *Increase faith* in the hearts of growing Christians
· *Inspire holiness* in the lives of believers
· *Instill hope* in the hearts of struggling people everywhere

Because He's coming again!

Published by Howard Books, a division of Simon & Schuster, Inc.
1230 Avenue of the Americas, New York, NY 10020
www.howardpublishing.com

The Best of Christmas in My Heart®, Volume 2 © 2008 by Joe Wheeler

Christmas in My Heart® is a registered trademark of Joe L. Wheeler,
and may not be used by anyone else in any form.
Visit Joe Wheeler's website at www.JoeWheelerBooks.com.

Representing the author is WordServe Literary Group, Ltd.,
10152 Knoll Circle, Highland Ranch, CO 80130.

The text or portions thereof are not to be reproduced
without written consent of the editor/compiler.

Library of Congress Cataloging-in-Publication Data
Christmas in my heart. Selections.
The best of Christmas in my heart / compiled and edited by Joe L. Wheeler.
p. cm.
1. Christmas stories, American. I. Wheeler, Joe L., 1936-
PS648.C45C4472 2007
813'.0108334—dc22
2007025637

ISBN-13: 978-1-4165-4678-8
ISBN-10:   1-4165-4678-2

1 3 5 7 9 10 8 6 4 2

HOWARD and colophon are registered trademarks of Simon & Schuster, Inc.

Manufactured in the United States of America

For information regarding special discounts for bulk purchases, please contact:
Simon & Schuster Special Sales at 1-800-456-6798 or business@simonandschuster.com.

Edited by Chrys Howard
Cover and interior design by Greg Jackson, Thinkpen Design, LLC., www.thinkpendesign.com

Table of Contents

LOVE AT CHRISTMAS

"Love at Christmas"—three little words, yet what magic there is in them! All the sentiment in the world encapsulated in those three words.

So how many of the Christmas stories I have been fortunate to collect are also love stories? I really had no idea. So I reached back through the years to 1992, when the *Christmas in My Heart®* series began, and then read forward through all 264 stories for an answer.

When I finished, I had discovered that over one-third could be loosely categorized as love stories, but not very many were love stories in the traditional sense: boy meets girl, girl is attracted to him, courtship results, complications arise, but love conquers all, and she accepts his proposal of marriage.

TWO DIFFERENT WORLDS

As I, for the very first time, assayed this mother lode of anthologized Christmas stories in the sixteen books, ever so gradually, like a negative developing in a darkroom tray, I saw an image coming into focus—an image of what is truly important in life and the realization that today's world needs these stories as a reminder.

The world today needs to be reminded that love should be pure and courtship should be lengthy; that the marriage ceremony should be moving, sacred, and for life, and intimacy saved for after marriage. Our world also needs to be reminded that marriage is the bedrock of society and family is the glue that holds the world together. The fact that *Christmas in My Heart®* is today the longest-running Christmas story series in America implies that the world likes to be reminded of these truths.

LOVE AT CHRISTMAS IN OUR STORIES

While it's true that the stories in my collections are not love stories in the traditional love story mode, they are love stories none-the-less. They are stories of love in marriages and families. They are stories of great triumph during times of trauma, of great joy in the face of despair, of great hope when times are hard.

These Christmas stories don't depict fairy-tale lives with perfect endings, they tell of real-life struggles that require families to bond together and grow closer. They reinforce the truth that families that stick together through good times and bad are ultimately the happiest. For it is not the size of the house or the size of the bank account that matters to a child—it is the strength of family that hovers around him through the delights and trials of every day.

Again and again, stories that touch the heart reinforce the concept that Christmas is not complete without children to share it with. The joy that comes from seeing a child's eyes light up on Christmas morning is a joy not to be missed. Children give us all a sense of purpose at Christmas time that we carry with us all year long.

Other than God, family is all we have to see us through, in our short tenure on this planet. The golden thread running through all these Christmas love stories is family. In truth, romancing one's family intensifies the love parents have for each other.

So what these Christmas love stories have to offer is this: through our children, our love for one another deepens. As time goes on, our love for our adult children continues to expand, and ultimately our love for our grandchildren becomes one of life's greatest serendipities—and Christmas is the catalyst for the greatest love story of all: Christ's birth in a Bethlehem manger.

Christmas Memories

THE LITTLEST ORPHAN AND THE CHRIST BABY

MARGARET E. SANGSTER, JR.

Life was bleak and full of pain for the Littlest Orphan. Now the one bright spot in his life—the picture of the Christ Baby—lay in splinters on the floor. With no mother to console him, and excluded from the celebration of Christmas, the Littlest Orphan now lay sobbing on his cot.

No story Margaret Sangster ever wrote is loved as much as this; it is generally considered to be one of the ten greatest Christmas stories ever written.

The Littlest Orphan gazed up into the face of the Christ Baby, who hung, gilt-framed and smiling, above the mantel-shelf. The mantel was dark, made of a black, mottled marble that suggested tombstones, and the long room—despite its rows of neat, white beds—gave an impression of darkness, too. But the picture above the mantel sparkled and scintillated and threw off an aura of sheer happiness. Even the neat "In Memoriam" card tacked to the wall directly under it could not detract from its joy. All of rosy babyhood, all of unspoiled laughter, all of the beginnings of life were in that picture! And the Littlest Orphan sensed it, even though he did not quite understand.

The Matron was coming down the room with many wreaths, perhaps a dozen of them, braceleting her thin arm. The wreaths were just a trifle dusty; their imitation holly leaves spoke plaintively of successive years of hard usage. But it was only two days before Christmas and the wreaths would not show up so badly under artificial light. The board of trustees, coming for the entertainment on Christmas Eve, never arrived until the early winter dusk had settled down. And the wreaths could be laid away, as soon as the holiday was past, for another twelve months.

The Littlest Orphan, staring up at the picture, did not hear the Matron's approaching footsteps. True, the Matron wore rubber heels—but any other orphan in the whole asylum would have heard her. Only the Littlest Orphan, with his thin, sensitive face and his curious fits of absorption, could have ignored her coming. He started painfully as her sharp voice cut into the silence.

"John," she said, and the frost that made such pretty lacework upon the window-pane wrought havoc with her voice, *"John, what are you doing here?"*

The Littlest Orphan answered after the manner of all small boy-children. "Nothin'!" he said.

Standing before him, the Matron—who was a large woman—seemed to tower. "You are not telling the truth, John," she said. "You have no right to be in the dormitory at this hour. Report to Miss Mace, at once" (Miss Mace was the primary teacher) "and tell her that I said you were to write five extra pages in your copybook. *At once!*"

With hanging head the Littlest Orphan turned away. It seemed terribly unfair, although it was against the rules to spend any but sleeping hours in the dormitory. He was just learning to write, and five pages meant a whole afternoon of cramped fingers and tired eyes. But how could he explain to this grim woman that the Christ Baby fascinated him, charmed him, and comforted him? How could he explain that the Christ Baby's wide eyes had a way of glancing down, almost with understanding, into his own? How could he tell, with the few weak words of his vocabulary, that he loved the Christ Baby whose smile was so tenderly sweet? That he spent much of his time standing, as he stood now, in the shadow of that smile?

He trudged away with never a word, down the length of the room, his clumsy shoes making a feeble clatter on the bare boards of the floor. When he was almost at the door, the Matron called after him.

"Don't drag your feet, John!" she commanded. And so he walked the rest of the way on tiptoe. And closed the door very softly after him.

The halls had already been decorated with long streamers of red and green crepe paper that looped along, in a half-hearted fashion, from picture to picture. The stair railing was wound with more of the paper, and the schoolroom—where Miss Mace sat stiffly behind a broad desk—was vaguely brightened by red cloth poinsettias set here and there at random. But the color of them was not reflected in the Littlest Orphan's heart, as he delivered his message and received in return a battered copybook.

As he sat at his desk, writing laboriously about the cat who ate the rat and the dog who ran after the cat, he could hear the other orphans playing outside in the courtyard. Always they played from four o'clock—when school was over—until five-thirty, which was suppertime. It was a rule to play from four until five-thirty. They were running and shouting together, but in a stilted way. The Littlest Orphan did not envy them much. They were all older and stronger than he, and their games were sometimes hard to enjoy. He had been the last baby taken before a new ruling making six years the minimum entrance age had gone through. And he was only five years old now. Perhaps it was his very littleness that made the Matron more intolerant of him—he presented to her a problem that could not be met in a mass way. His clothing had to be several sizes smaller than the other clothing; his lessons less advanced. And so on.

Drearily he wrote. And listened, between sentences, to the scratching pen of Miss Mace. . . . The dog had caught the cat. And now the man beat the dog. And then it was time to start all over again, back at the place where the cat ate the rat. Two pages, three pages, four pages. . . . Surreptitiously the Littlest Orphan moved his fingers, one by one, and wondered that he was still able to move them. Then, working slowly, he finished the last page and handed the copybook back to the teacher. As she studied it, her face softened slightly.

"Why did the Matron punish you, John?" she asked, as if on impulse, as she made a correction in a sentence.

The Littlest Orphan hesitated for a second. And then: "I shouldn't have been in th' dormitory," he said slowly. "An' I was!"

Again Miss Mace asked a question.

"But what," she queried, "were you doing there? Why weren't you out playing with the other children?"

She didn't comment upon the fault, but the Littlest Orphan knew that she, also, thought the punishment rather severe. Only it isn't policy to criticize a superior's method of discipline. He answered her second question gravely.

"I was lookin' at th' Christ Baby over the mantel," he said.

As if to herself, Miss Mace spoke. "You mean the picture Mrs. Benchly gave in memory of her son" she murmured, "the pastel." And then, "Why were you looking at it—" She hesitated, and the Littlest Orphan didn't know that she had almost said "dear."

Shyly the child spoke, and wistfulness lay across his thin, small face—an unrealized wistfulness. "He looks so—nice—" said the Littlest Orphan gently, "like he had a mother, maybe."

Supper that night was brief, and after supper there were carols to practice in the assembly room. The Littlest Orphan, seated at the extreme end of the line, enjoyed the singing. The red-headed boy, who fought so often in the courtyard, had a high, thrilling soprano. Listening to him, as he sang the solo parts, made the Littlest Orphan forget a certain black eye—and a nose that had once been swollen and bleeding. Made him forget lonely hours when he had lain uncomforted in his bed—as a punishment for quarreling.

The red-headed boy was singing something about "gold and frank-kin-sense and myrrh." The Littlest Orphan told himself that they must be very beautiful things. Gold—the Christ Baby's frame was of gold—but frank-kin-sense and myrrh were unguessed names. Maybe they were flowers—real flowers that smelled pretty, not red cloth ones. He shut his eyes, singing automatically, and imagined what these flowers looked like—the color and shape of their petals, and whether they grew on tall lily stalks or on short pansy stems. And then the singing was over, and he opened his eyes with a start and realized that the Matron was speaking.

"Before you go to bed," she was saying, "I want you to understand that you must be on your good behavior until after the trustees leave tomorrow evening. You must not make any disorder in the corridors or in the dormitories—they have been especially cleaned and dusted. You must pay strict attention to the singing; the trustees like to hear you sing! They will all be here—even Mrs. Benchly, who has not visited us since her son died. And if one of you misbehaves—"

She stopped abruptly, but her silence was crowded with meaning, and many a child squirmed uncomfortably in his place. It was only after a moment that she spoke again.

"Good-night!" she said abruptly.

And the orphans chorused back, "Good-night."

Undressing carefully and swiftly, for the dormitory was cold and the lights were dim, the Littlest Orphan wondered about the trustees—and in particular about the Mrs. Benchly who had lost her son. All trustees were ogres to asylum children, but the Littlest Orphan couldn't help feeling that Mrs. Benchly was the least ogre-like of them all. Somehow she was a part of the Christ Baby's picture, and it was a part of her. If she were responsible for it, she could not be all bad! So ruminating, the Littlest Orphan said his brief prayers—any child who forgot his prayers was punished severely—and slid between the sheets into his bed.

Some of the orphans made a big lump under their bed-covers. The red-headed boy was stocky, and so were others. Some of them were almost fat. But the Littlest Orphan made hardly any lump at all. The sheet, the cotton blanket, and the spread went over him with scarcely a ripple. Often the Littlest Orphan had wished that there might be another small boy who could share his bed—he took up such a tiny section of it. Another small boy would have made the bed seem warmer, somehow, and less lonely. Once two orphans had come to the asylum, and they were brothers. They had shared things—beds and desks and books. Maybe brothers were unusual gifts from a surprisingly blind providence, gifts that were granted only once in a hundred years! More rare, even, than mothers.

Mothers—the sound of the word had a strange effect upon the Littlest Orphan, even when he said it silently in his soul. It meant so much that he did not comprehend—so much for which he vaguely hungered. Mothers stood for warm arms, and kisses, and soft words. Mothers meant punishments, too, but gentle punishment that did not really come from way inside.

Often the Littlest Orphan had heard the rest talking stealthily about mothers. Some of them could actually remember having owned one! But the Littlest Orphan could not remember. He had arrived at the asylum as a baby—delicate and frail and too young for memories that would later come to bless him and to cause a strange, sharp sort of hurt. When the rest spoke of bedtime stories, and lullabies, and sugar cookies, he listened—wide-eyed and half-incredulous—to their halting sentences.

It was growing very cold in the dormitory, and it was dark. Even the faint flicker of light had been taken away. The Littlest Orphan wiggled his toes, under the cotton blanket, and wished that sleep would come. Some nights it came quickly, but this night—perhaps he was overtired, and it was so cold!

As a matter of habit his eyes searched through the dark for the place where the Christ Baby hung. He could not distinguish even the dim outlines of the gilt frame, but he knew that the Christ Baby was rosy and chubby and smiling—that his eyes were deeply blue and filled with cheer. Involuntarily the Littlest Orphan stretched out his thin hands and dropped them back again against the spread. All about him the darkness lay like a smothering coat, and the Christ Baby, even though he smiled, was invisible. The other children were sleeping. All up and down the long room sounded their regular breathing, but the Littlest Orphan could not sleep. He wanted something that he was unable to define—wanted it with such a burning intensity that the tears crowded into his eyes. He sat up abruptly in his bed—a small, shivering figure with quivering lips and a baby ache in his soul that had never really known babyhood.

Loneliness—it swept about him. More disheartening than the cold. More enveloping than the darkness. There was no fear in him of the shadows in the corner, of the creaking shutters and the narrow stair. Such fears are discouraged early in children who live by rule and routine. No—it was a feeling more poignant than fear—a feeling that clutched at him and squeezed his small body until it was dry and shaking and void of expression.

Of all the sleeping dormitory the Littlest Orphan was the only child who knew the ache of such loneliness. Even the ones who had been torn away from family ties had, each one of them, something beautiful to keep preciously close. But the Littlest Orphan had nothing—nothing. . . . The loneliness filled him with a strange impulse, an impulse that sent him sliding over the edge of his bed with small arms outflung.

All at once he was crossing the floor on bare, mouse-quiet feet. Past the placidly sleeping children, past the row of lockers, past the table with its neat cloth and black-bound, impressive guest-book. Past everything until he stood, a white spot in the blackness, directly under the mantel. The Christ Baby hung above him. And, though the Littlest Orphan could not see, he felt that the blue eyes were looking down tenderly. All at once he wanted to touch the Christ Baby, to hold him tight, to feel the sweetness and warmth of him. Tensely, still moved by the curious impulse, he tiptoed back to where the table stood. Carefully he laid the guest-book on the floor; carefully he removed the white cloth. And then staggering under the—to him—great weight, he carried the table noiselessly back with him. Though it was really a small, light table, the Littlest Orphan breathed hard as he set it down. He had to rest, panting, for a moment, before he could climb up on it.

All over the room lay silence, broken only by the sleepy sounds of the children. The Littlest Orphan listened almost prayerfully as he clambered upon the table top and drew himself to an erect position. His small hands groped along the mantel shelf, touched the lower edge of the gilt frame. But the Christ Baby was still out of reach.

Feverishly, obsessed with one idea, the Littlest Orphan raised himself on tiptoe. His hands gripped the chill marble of the mantel. Tugging, twisting—all with the utmost quiet—he pulled himself up until he was kneeling upon the mantel shelf. Quivering with nervousness as well as the now intense cold, he finally stood erect. And then—only then—he was able to feel the wire and nail that held the Christ Baby's frame against the wall. His numb fingers loosened the wire carefully. And then at last the picture was in his arms.

It was heavy, the picture. And hard. Not soft and warm as he had somehow expected it to be. But it was the Christ Baby nevertheless. Holding it close, the Littlest Orphan fell to speculating upon the ways of getting down, now that both of his hands were occupied. It would be hard to slide from the mantel to the table, and from table to floor, with neither sound nor mishap.

His eyes troubled, his mouth a wavering line in his pinched face, the Littlest Orphan crowded back against the wall. The darkness held now the vague menace of depth. Destruction lurked in a single misstep. It had been a long way up. It would be even longer going down. And he now had the Christ Baby, as well as himself, to care for.

Gingerly he advanced one foot over the edge of the mantel—and drew it back. Sharply. He almost screamed in sudden terror. It was as if the dark had reached out long, bony fingers to pull him from his place of safety. He wanted to raise his hands to his face—but he could not release his hold upon the gilt frame. All at once he realized that his hands were growing numb with the cold and that his feet were numb, too.

The minutes dragged by. Somewhere a clock struck—many times. The Littlest Orphan had never heard the clock strike so many times, at night, before. He cowered back until it seemed to his scared, small mind that he would sink into the wall. And then, as the clock ceased striking, he heard another sound—a sound that brought dread to his heart. It was a step in the hall, a heavy, firm step that—despite rubber heels—as now clearly recognizable. It would be the Matron, making her rounds of the building before she went to bed. As the steps came nearer along the hall, a light, soft and yellow, seemed to grow in the place. It would be the lamp that she carried in her hand.

The Matron reached the door—peered in. And then, with lamp held high, she entered the room. And her swift glance swept the rows of white beds—each, but one, with its sleeping occupant.

The Littlest Orphan, on the mantel, clutched the Christ Baby closer in his arms. And waited. It seemed to him that his shivering must shake the room. He gritted his teeth convulsively, as the Matron's eyes found his tumbled, empty bed.

Hastily, forgetting to be quiet, the woman crossed the room. She pulled back the spread, the blanket. And then—as if drawn by a magnet—her eyes lifted, traveled across the room. And found the small, white figure that pressed back into the narrow space. Her voice was sharper even than her eyes, when she spoke.

"John," she called abruptly—and her anger made her forget to be quiet—*"What are you doing up there?"*

Across the top of the Christ Baby's gilt frame, the eyes of the Littlest Orphan stared into the eyes of the Matron with something of the fascination that one sees in the eyes of a bird charmed by a cat or a snake. In narrow, white beds, all over the room, children were stirring, pulling themselves erect, staring. One child snickered behind a sheltering hand. But the Littlest Orphan was conscious only of the Matron. He waited for her to speak again. In a moment she did.

"John," she said, and her voice was burning, and yet chill, with rage, *"you are a bad boy. Come down at once!"*

His eyes blank with sheer fright, his arms clasping the picture close—The Littlest Orphan answered the tone of that voice. With quivering lips he advanced one foot, then the other. And stepped into the space that was the room below. He was conscious that some child screamed—he, himself, did not utter a sound. And that the Matron started forward. And then he struck the table and rolled with it, and the Christ Baby's splintering picture, into the darkness.

The Littlest Orphan spent the next day in bed, with an aching head and a wounded heart. The pain of his bruises did not make a great difference; neither did the threats of the Matron penetrate his consciousness. Only the bare space over the mantel mattered—only the blur of blue and yellow and red upon the hearth, where the pastel had struck. Only the knowledge that the Christ Baby—the meaning of all light and happiness—was no more, troubled him.

There was a pleasant stir about the asylum. An excited child, creeping into the dormitory, told the Littlest Orphan that one of the trustees had sent a tree. And that another was donating ice cream. And that there were going to be presents. But the Littlest Orphan did not even smile. His wan face was set and drawn. Dire punishment waited him after his hurts were healed. And there would be no Christ Baby to go to for comfort and cheer when the punishment was over.

The morning dragged on. Miss Mace brought his luncheon of bread and milk and was as kind to him as she dared to be—your Miss Maces have been made timorous by a too forceful world. Once, during the early afternoon, the Matron came in to examine his bruised head, and once a maid came to rub the colored stains from the hearth. The Littlest Orphan caught his breath as he watched her. And then it began to grow dark, and the children were brought upstairs to be washed and dressed in clean blouses for the entertainment. They had been warned not to talk with him, and they obeyed—for there were folk watching and listening. But even so, flickers of conversation—excited, small-boy conversation—drifted to the Littlest Orphan's waiting ears. Someone had said there was to be a Santa Claus. In a red suit and a white beard. Perhaps—it was true. The Littlest Orphan slid down under the covers and pulled the sheet high over his aching head. He didn't want the rest to know that he was crying.

The facewashing was accomplished swiftly. Just as swiftly were the blouses adjusted to the last tie, string, and button. And then the children filed downstairs, and the Littlest Orphan was left alone again. He pulled himself up gingerly until he sat erect, and buried his face in his hands.

Suddenly, from downstairs, came the sound of music. First, the tiny piano, and then the voices of the children as they sang. Automatically the Littlest Orphan joined in, his voice quavering weakly through the empty place. He didn't want to sing—there was neither rhythm nor melody in his heart. But he had been taught to sing those songs, and sing them he must.

First there was "O Little Town of Bethlehem." And then a carol. And then the one about "Gold and frank-kin-sense and myrrh." Strange that the words did not mean flowers tonight! And then there was a hush—perhaps it was a prayer. And then a burst of clapping and a jumble of glad cries. Perhaps that was the Santa Claus in his trappings of white and scarlet. The Littlest Orphan's tears came like hot rain to his tired eyes.

There was a sound in the hall. A rubber-heeled step upon the bare floor. The Littlest Orphan slid down again under the covers, until only the bandage on the brow was at all visible. When the Matron stooped over him, she could not even glimpse his eyes. With a vigorous hand she jerked aside the covers.

"Sick or no," she told him, "you've got to come downstairs. Mrs. Benchly wants to see the boy who broke her son's memorial picture. I'll help you with your clothes."

Trembling violently, the Littlest Orphan allowed himself to be wedged into undies and a blouse and a pair of coarse, dark trousers. He laced his shoes with fingers that shook with mingled fear and weakness. And then he followed the Matron out of the dormitory and through the long halls, with their mocking festoons of red and green crepe paper, and into the assembly room where the lights were blinding and the Christmas tree was a blaze of glory.

The trustees sat at one end of the room, the far end. They were a mass of dark colors, blacks and browns and somber grays. Following in the wake of the Matron, the Littlest Orphan stumbled toward them. Mrs. Benchly—would she beat him in front of all the rest? Would she leap at him accusingly from that dark mass? He felt smaller than he had ever felt before, and more inadequate.

The children were beginning to sing again. But despite their singing, the Matron spoke. Not loudly, as she did to the children, but with a curious deference.

"This is John, Mrs. Benchly," she said, "the child who broke the picture."

Biting his lips, so that he would not cry out, the Littlest Orphan stood in the vast shadow of the Matron. He shut his eyes. Perhaps if this Mrs. Benchly meant to strike him, it would be best to have his eyes shut. And then suddenly a voice came, a voice so soft that somehow he could almost feel the velvet texture of it.

"Poor child," said the voice, "he's frightened. And ill, too. Come here, John. I won't hurt you, dear."

Opening his eyes incredulously, the Littlest Orphan stared past the Matron into the sort of face small children dream about. Violet-eyed and tender. Lined, perhaps, and sad about the mouth, and wistful. But so sweet! Graying hair, with a bit of a wave in it, brushed back from a broad, white brow. And slim, white, reaching hands. The Littlest Orphan went forward without hesitation. Something about this lady was reminiscent of the Christ Baby. As her white hand touched his, tightened on it, he looked up into her face with the ghost of a smile.

The children had crowded almost informally to the other end of the room, toward the tree. The dark mass of the trustees was dissolving, breaking up into fragments, that followed the children. One of the trustees laughed aloud. Not at all like an ogre. A sudden sense of gladness began—for no understandable reason—to steal across the Littlest Orphan's consciousness. Rudely the voice of the Matron broke in upon it.

"I had warned the children," she said, "not to disturb anything. Last evening, before they retired. John deliberately disobeyed. And the picture is ruined in consequence. What do you think we had better do about it, Mrs. Benchly?"

For a moment the lady with the dream face did not speak. She was drawing the Littlest Orphan nearer, until he touched the satin folds of her black gown. And despite the Matron's voice, he was not afraid. When at last she answered the Matron, he did not flinch.

"I think," she said gently, "that I'll ask you to leave us. I would like to talk with John—alone."

And, as the Matron walked stiffly away, down the length of the room, she lifted the Littlest Orphan into her lap.

"I know," she said, and her voice was even gentler than it had been, "that you didn't mean to break the picture. Did you, dear?"

Eagerly the Littlest Orphan answered, "Oh, no—ma'am!" he told her. I didn't mean t' break th' Christ Baby."

The woman's arms were about him. They tightened suddenly. "You're so young," she said; "you're such a mite of a thing. I doubt if you could understand why I had the picture made. Why I gave it to the home here, to be hung in the dormitory. . . . My little son was all I had after my husband died. And his nursery—it was such a pretty room—had a Christ Child picture on the wall. And my boy always loved the picture. . . . And so when he—left—" her voice faltered, "I had an artist copy it. I—I couldn't part with the original! And I sent it to a place where there would be many small boys, who could enjoy it as my son had always—" Her voice broke.

The Littlest Orphan stared in surprise at the lady's face. Her violet eyes were misted like April blossoms with the dew upon them. Her lips quivered. Could it be that she, too, was lonesome and afraid? His hand crept up until it touched her soft cheek.

"I *loved* th' Christ Baby," he said simply.

The lady looked at him. With an effort she downed the quaver in her voice. "I can't believe," she said at last, "that you destroyed the picture purposely. No matter what she"—her glance rested upon the Matron's stiff figure, half a room away—"may think! John, dear, did you mean to spoil the gift I gave—in my small boy's name? Oh—I'm sure you didn't."

All day long the Littlest Orphan had lived in fear and agony of soul. All day long he had known pain—physical pain and the pain of suspense. Suddenly he buried his face in the lady's neck—he had never known before that there was a place in ladies' necks, just made for tiny heads—and the tears came. Choked by sobs, he spoke.

"No'm," he sobbed, "I didn't mean to. . . . It was only because I was cold. And lonesome. An' th' bed was—big. An' all th' rest was asleep. An' the Christ Baby always looked so pink . . . an' glad . . . an' warm. An' I wanted t' take him inter my bed. An' cuddle close!" he burrowed his head deeper into the neck—"so that I wouldn't be cold any more. Or lonesome—any more."

The lady's arms tightened about the Littlest Orphan's body until the pressure almost hurt—but it was a nice sort of hurt. It shocked her, somehow, to feel the thinness of that body. And her tears fell quite unrestrained upon the Littlest Orphan's bandaged head. And then all at once she bent over. And her lips pressed, ever so tenderly, upon the place where his cheek almost met her ear.

"Not to be cold," she whispered, more to herself than to the Littlest Orphan, "or lonesome any more! To have the nursery opened again—and the sound of the tiny feet in the empty rooms. To have the Christ Child smiling down upon a sleeping little boy. To kiss bruises away again. . . . Not to be lonesome any more, or cold—"

Suddenly she tilted back the Littlest Orphan's head; was looking deep, deep into his bewildered eyes.

"John," she said, and his name sounded so different when she said it—"how would you like to come away from here, and live in my house, with me? How would you like to be my boy?"

A silence had crept over the other end of the room. One of the trustees, who wore a clerical collar, had mounted the platform. He was reading from the Bible that visiting ministers read from of a Sunday. His voice rang—resonant and rich as an organ tone—through the room.

"For unto us a child is born," he read, "unto us a son is given."

The Littlest Orphan, with a sigh of utter happiness, crowded closer into the arms that held him.

And it was Christmas Eve!

•

Margaret E. Sangster, Jr., (1894–1981) was an editor, scriptwriter, journalist, short-story writer, and novelist. She was one of the most beloved inspirational writers of the first half of the twentieth century.

THE YULE MIRACLE

ALBERT PAYSON TERHUNE

"No brains. No courage. No affection. Nothing but bigness and appetite." That was Yule, the beautiful collie the entire family had given up on. But even Karen, Yule's owner, deep down, despaired of ever seeing signs of intelligence in her dog.

It was a pretty trick which Karen Brayle had taught her Christmas collie. She and the dog had happened upon the game by accident. Thereafter, they played it a hundred times, when they were alone together.

Indeed, it was almost the only thing she or anyone else had ever been able to teach the big, lumbering young dog. So Karen was the prouder of it. But, always fearing the puppy would get stage fright and humiliate her if she should attempt to play it with him in public, she contented herself with private performances.

Nor did she brag of the collie's single achievement, lest incredulous hearers insist on her proving its truth; and lest the dog add to his unpopularity in the family by flunking the test.

On the Christmas Eve before, Mr. Brayle had brought home the huge leggy young dog as a Yule gift to his only daughter. Karen had been rapturously happy over the present. In memory of the day, she had named her gift "Yule"; a short and easy name to call him by, but a name to which he did not respond unless he felt inclined to.

The young collie had been beautiful in golden coat and unduly large in bone. The deep set, dark eyes should have held a blend of mischievousness and sternness. Instead, the expression was merely foolish. Yes, that was the keynote of Yule's nature. He seemed incurably foolish.

Karen found this out before he had been in the house a day. So did the entire Brayle family—Karen's father and mother and her two older brothers. One and all, they had read and had heard of the uncannily keen brain power of collies, of the breed's loyalty and chumship. Great things had they expected from this overgrown pedigreed pup. And not a thing did they get.

It was as though people had paid a stiff price to see the tragedy of *Hamlet* and had found a slapstick film substituted for the Shakespeare play, or had gone to an Einstein lecture and been confronted by the village idiot.

Nothing did the bumble-puppy collie know, and nothing did he seem able to learn. The more they worked with him, the duller he seemed to become. He had a genius for getting into the house and ripping rugs to rags and disemboweling overstuffed chairs and yanking down window curtains. But he could not be taught to obey or even to answer to his name.

He was a pest, a nuisance, a dead loss.

At first the Brayles were dazed with incredulous surprise at the silliness of the collie from which they had hoped so much. Then they piled derisively disgusted epithets on him, and accepted Yule as a mighty bad joke on themselves.

All but Karen.

Even as a mother often feels more tenderness for some crippled or dull child than for her normal offspring, so the sneering ridicule of her parents and brothers made Karen cling more lovingly to poor brainless Yule.

This although she knew better than did anyone else how utterly worthless the dog was. It was she, for instance, who undertook to train him, and who plumbed the total lack of his intelligence to its depths. It was she who, on one of their first walks together, witnessed the humiliating scene when a miniature-size Pomeranian growled at the shambling golden giant and Yule fled howling under the nearest porch, at the tiny lapdog's attack.

"No brains," mused Karen. "No courage. No affection. Nothing but bigness and appetite. That's you, poor Yule."

The dog thumped his tail on the floor as she spoke. She thrilled in hope it meant he recognized his name at last. But he was only wagging his plumed tail because he saw the cook drawing near with his basinful of dinner scraps. Almost fiercely, Karen threw her arms around the shaggy neck, and hugged the vacuously grinning Yule to her heart.

"Never mind!" she consoled him—though he stood in scant need of consolation and was far more interested in the approaching dinner basin than in his young owner. "Never mind, Yule! I love you better than I love anyone else except the family. I don't know why, but I do. You can be as stupid as you like. I'll keep on loving you, just the same—"

She broke off in her crooned whisper of comfort, because Yule tore loose from her arms and went charging clumsily at the basin the cook was carrying to him. Karen left him in disgust. In spite of the care she had spent on him, the poor puppy seemed as hopelessly silly as ever.

It was during the first warm week of spring that Karen discovered the dog's only trick, the one I have spoken of. By that time, the girl was the sole member of the household who would so much as glance at Yule, much less speak to him. The rest were thoroughly disgusted with him. But for Karen's affection for the uncouth creature, he would have been packed off, long before.

By the time the winter ice broke up in the lake a furlong from the Brayle home, Karen had taken Yule to the water to teach him to swim. To her disappointment, though not to her surprise, the collie refused to go into the lake to any depth farther than his own mid-legs. There, before the water could reach as high as his stomach, he would recoil, tail between legs, and run ki-yi-ing to the shore. (This, by the way, was not necessarily a part of his normal cowardly idiocy. Not one collie in five enjoys swimming or will go voluntarily out of his depth in water. But not one collie in ninety will ki-yi, or show other abject signs of terror when he is urged into the deeps.)

The first day of the season when she was allowed to go swimming, Karen ran down the beach with Yule capering and barking alongside. When she was ankle-deep in the lake, she stumbled. Seeking to right herself, she lurched sidewise and fell prone on her face in a few inches of water.

Instantly, Yule's fanfare of barking swelled tenfold. He charged over to the prostrate girl. Seizing her by one shoulder of her bathing suit, he dug his teeth deep into the cloth and braced his four feet, hauling backward with all his strength, to drag her to land.

Karen was overjoyed at this manifestation of the lifesaving instinct. She praised Yule loudly and effusively, patting and lauding him until he danced in ungainly pride.

Twice more, in succession, the girl ran down the beach and fell sidewise into the shallow water. Each time Yule rushed barking after her and sought to haul her ashore. Each time he was praised as fulsomely as at first. He waxed vastly proud of himself, vanity being the one salient collie trait he had thus far developed.

Then came the real test, a test which Karen approached without a qualm of misgiving, a test which would give her something to boast of at home and which could not fail to boost Yule's stock with the whole disapproving family.

She dashed down the beach afresh. But this time she did not fall prostrate in eight inches of water. Instead, she kept on, until no longer could she feel the lake pebbles under her feet. Then, throwing herself on one side she began to flounder and to call to Yule for help.

As a matter of fact, Karen was about as much in danger of drowning as would be a duck which is tossed into a pond. Almost from babyhood she had been an expert swimmer. But she gave a really creditable imitation of a drowning person. All the while, she watched with one eye the big golden collie on the beach behind her.

Let Yule once plunge into the lake and swim out to her and catch her by the shoulder and try to pull her ashore, and she would know he had the true collie soul, the clean white heart which will risk death to save a loved human being. Eagerly she waited, redoubling her splashing and her calls for help.

Yule raced up and down the bank, barking in asinine futility, once or twice venturing out into perhaps twelve inches of water and then shrinking back to shore to recommence his deafening idiotic barks. He was giving a magnificent exhibition of panic-stricken uselessness, and his every movement showed he lacked any of the pluck needed to go to his supposedly drowning mistress' rescue.

Disillusioned, cruelly chagrined, Karen swam shoreward and climbed the beach. Yule met her, ecstatically, as though congratulating her on her lucky escape from death. For a moment she glared angrily down upon the capering dog. Then she stopped and patted him.

"Poor worthless Yule!" she exclaimed, with more tenderness than contempt in her voice. "You can't help being what you are. None of us can. And perhaps somewhere there are collies like the ones in the stories. It isn't your fault you're not one of them. I love you, anyhow, if nobody else does."

Daily, after that, at the outset of her swim, Karen and Yule went through that mock lifesaving stunt, in water eight inches deep. The sport never palled on the young dog. Indeed he became more and more dexterous at it, learning to take better grip and to use wiser leverage.

But ever, when Karen swam out into the lake, the collie remained timorously behind. Try as she would, Karen could not coax him into deep water. When she pretended to be in distress, he would bark plangently and run up and down the beach. But not once did he venture out to her aid. In short, he was an ideal lifesaver, as long as he could enact the role without getting wet or risking a swim.

Karen loved him for what he was. Not for what she had hoped he might be. Nobody else loved him at all. None of the Brayles could endure the sight of the clumsy clown collie. Much teasing from her brothers and many a sour look from her father did Karen endure because of her silly golden comrade.

The long summer drowsed away. Autumn brought V-shaped cohorts of wild geese flying southward across the lake. Winter set in.

Karen and Yule still were inseparable comrades, till the girl went to school. But Karen had given up trying to ding sense into the collie's thick head. She accepted him for a stupid and bumptious and beautiful plaything.

Meanwhile, the passing year had brought depth to Yule's chest and grace to his limbs and a massiveness to his heavy gold and white coat. Ignorant of collies, the Brayles scarcely noted these very gradual physical changes, nor did they bother to guess whether or not age was working similar development to the dog's soul and brain.

The fox terrier puppy at six months old, is graceful and fleet. The lion cub, at the same age, is gawkily helpless. Thackeray was a giant. As a boy he was rated a lazy fool. Bismarck was a giant. As a boy, he could not so much as master his lessons and later was dropped from college. The boy Lincoln was shambling and physically lazy.

But if the Brayles had heard of these cases of the slow development of giants, they most assuredly did not apply the rule to the gigantic collie they despised.

Christmas was drawing near. There was no more promise of a white and icy Christmas that year than that Yule would turn into a prodigy. The dank chill of November continued to hang over the land, without merging into the tingling cold of late December.

As a general thing, long before Christmas, the lake was several inches thick in glass-clear ice and the hills were glittering with deep snow. But now the ice merely formed in a skim along the shore. The land lay glumly gray-brown and snowless. There could scarcely have been less appropriate Christmastide weather or scenery.

Karen came home for the holidays to be greeted rapturously and loudly by Yule. For her sake the collie had been tolerated during her absence.

The morning after her return, her father called her into his study. He and she were alone in the house at the moment, except for the collie, which Mr Brayle shoved impatiently from the room as Yule strove to follow Karen thither.

"Listen, daughter," began Mr. Brayle, without preamble. "All of us want you to be happy. You know that. We want you to have the very happiest Christmas we can give you. But—"

"But what, Daddy?" asked Karen, puzzled.

"But that's just what we tried to do for you last year," pursued her father. "That's why we bought Yule for you. And look how he's turned out! I'd call him an unmitigated nuisance if I weren't afraid of doing rank injustice to some real unmitigated nuisance. That's what I want to talk to you about this morning."

"But I love Yule," protested Karen. "He and I—"

"You mean you love all animals. Yule is the only animal you've ever played around with, so you think you're fond of him," corrected Mr. Brayle. "Now here is my idea. For one solid year we've put up with that fool dog. We have been the laughing-stock of the people on both sides of us. He hasn't a scrap of intelligence or of loyalty or of companionableness. He's a one million per cent failure. He—"

"But I—"

"Wait a minute. I know a man who will take him off our hands. He says he'll give him a good home in the city. He lives alone in a flat there, and he wants some companion to welcome him home at night. I didn't tell the man quite what a fool the collie is. He'll find that out soon enough. But I told him I'd try to get you to consent to part with Yule. If you will, daughter, I've a chance to buy you a splendid well-trained clever Boston terrier in his place. The Boston can be delivered here Christmas morning. It's up to you. What do you say?"

For a long half minute, Karen Brayle faced her father. She felt she was growing red and redder, and an unbidden mist began to creep in front of her unhappy eyes. Patiently, Mr. Brayle waited for her to speak. He seemed relieved to have said his say. At last Karen spoke. Fast she spoke, and with growing speed and incoherence.

"I love Yule," she repeated. "And he loves me. I know that. But even if I didn't care anything about him, I'd rather see him shot than sent to a little flat in a big city. He'd have to spend the whole day in a space no bigger than our porch here all alone and wondering why I deserted him."

Despite her self-control, something had risen in her throat that threatened to choke her. Now, lest she disgrace her sixteen years of age by tears, Karen turned abruptly and fled from the room. Mr. Brayle watched with worried face as he saw her run out of the house and along the sloping hillside below.

Mr. Brayle sighed, and was about to turn away when his gaze focused on the girl.

In her aimless craving to be alone, Karen Brayle had unconsciously taken the hillside path which led down to the lake edge to the pier which jutted out into deep water. Out onto the ice-slippery pier she made her blind way. At its string-piece, she checked her haste. At least, she strove to. It was then that her father's idly sympathetic gaze turned sharp and worried.

Karen's smooth-soled house shoes slid along a swath of ice which had formed.

She strove vainly for her balance, lurched forward, her feet going suddenly from under her—and slid off the edge of the string-piece and thence down into twelve feet of ice-strewn water.

Mr. Brayle shouted in impotent terror. Bursting out of the house, he ran down the slope at blundering speed. Not that he feared Karen would drown, despite her thick clothing, but lest the wintry ducking give her pneumonia. Immersion in such icy water, followed by a buffeting from the cold morning wind, might well make her gravely ill.

Mr. Brayle himself had never bothered to learn to swim. He had envied his daughter her skill in the water. But he'd not envied her enough to learn the same art. He was running down to the pier simply that he might wrap her in his heavy dressing-gown when she should emerge.

Then his pace quickened, and his face went rigid. For, as Karen struck out, he saw her double up and claw helplessly at the water with constricted fingers.

Nervous excitement and the dive into the bitterly cold water had sent a cramp through every inch of her athletic body. Her legs and arms contracted in anguish.

Mr. Brayle yelled for help as he ran. But he knew how useless was the shout. His wife and sons had driven to the nearby village. There was no human being within a mile.

Then, whizzing past him like a flung spear, something big and golden dashed at express train speed toward the lake.

Onto the pier flew Yule. At the string-piece, the collie launched himself outward, with no shadow of hesitation, into space. His shaggy body smote the water, not a yard from the sinking girl, and immediately his mighty jaws seized the shoulder of her stout sweater.

Then, heading instinctively toward the strip of beach below the pier, Yule towed the knotted and impotent girl toward shore. Inch by inch the dog beat his way shoreward, tugging with him the adored mistress whom so often he had hauled playfully along in shallow water.

Karen's feet grated against the pebbles of the shoal. Her father rushed out, knee deep into the chill water, and snatched her in his arms. Already her father had wrapped Karen in his thick dressing gown and was running as fast as he possibly could with her toward the house. Yule loped easily after them.

An hour later, after a vigorous rub-down with a crash towel and a still more vigorous alcohol rub, Karen sat in a big chair in her father's study, her feet to the fire, her parents and brothers gathering about her.

In the midst of her oft-repeated story of the rescue, Yule walked into the room. Majestically, he strode up to his young mistress and laid his classic head on her knee.

A moment's silence fell upon the group. All of them were staring dumbly at the huge collie. It was Mr. Brayle who spoke.

"Look!" he bade the rest. "Look at those eyes! What has become of their flat silliness? See! The true 'look of eagles' is lurking behind them. He's—he's a *dog!* Not a clown any more."

"It was there all the time," said Karen, gathering the splendid head tightly into her embrace. "More and more it was there. But something had to be worn away by time or else snatched away by a shock, to change him from a big puppy to a great dog. It's *happened*. Do you still want to swap him for a terrier, Daddy?" she added mischievously.

Mr. Brayle shuddered. Slowly he crossed to where Yule stood close beside Karen's deep chair. Half hesitantly the man held out one hand, as if in propitiation.

"Yule," he said humbly, "I apologize. No other dog is ever going to replace you here, as long as I live. Will you shake on it?"

Gravely, with an air of perfect equality, Yule laid one white forepaw into the man's outstretched palm.

"We've got a Christmas collie at last," remarked Mr. Brayle, his other hand lying on the dog's silken head. "A perfect Christmas collie. One year behind schedule."

•

Albert Payson Terhune (1872–1942) was one of the most popular writers of his time, writing hundreds of articles and short stories (mostly having to do with dogs) as well as around forty books (both fiction and nonfiction).

Christmas Memories

UNDER THE BANANA LEAF CHRISTMAS TREE

CAROLYN RATHBUN-SUTTON

It's easy to get into the Christmas mood when church bells are ringing, when bright lights shed a radiance on the evergreen Christmas tree, and when snow is flocking the entire world outside. But what if you're half a world away in unrelenting heat, jungle drums are beating, and all you have is a pathetic-looking banana leaf Christmas tree?

Carolyn Rathbun-Sutton vividly remembers one such Christmas.

Carefully I tied a red bow around the neck of our German shepherd puppy. The kitten would be next, if I could catch her. As I slid two pans of cinnamon rolls onto the lower rack of the wood-burning oven, I couldn't help wishing that it felt more like Christmas. But with the banana plantation just outside the window, it was hard to get into the spirit of things.

Only three months before, my husband and I had begun our first school year teaching in Africa. How slowly those months were passing! Furlough was still two years and nine months away.

A streak of black fur dashed past the refrigerator. Despite her squirming protests, I tied a Christmas bow about the kitten's neck.

The windup timer finally buzzed; the cinnamon rolls were ready. Ah, something special to eat! I was determined Christmas wouldn't be the disaster our first Thanksgiving had been.

Thanksgiving Day a month before had found us both in bed with high fevers from a particularly severe strain of flu raging through the isolated mountains of northern Zaire. While the Voice of America radio announcer—sounding much like my father—had explained the family significance of Thanksgiving to listeners around the world, I had quietly hid my heavily flowing tears under Grandmother's quilt. That is, until I heard my husband drop his face into a pillow and begin sobbing. Home was still on the other side of the world.

HOLIDAY PREPARATIONS

How do you generate a cozy Christmas mood when jungle drums are beating in the village across the road, a warm breeze is rustling nearby palm leaves, and the broken school generator won't let you play Christmas carols on the phonograph? How do you buy Christmas gifts when your first salary check is four months overdue?

But planning ahead for the holidays, I'd borrowed enough money to pay our only American neighbors to bring me chocolate chips, cinnamon, and powdered sugar from Kampala, Uganda, 17 hours away. And from a small lemon a child had sold me at the front door, I had squeezed enough juice for two tiny tarts—which would be Christmas dinner's centerpiece.

Along the mantel, I finished hanging the few ornaments our two-year-old family owned. They reflected the flames of an unnecessary fire. Under the makeshift banana-leaf Christmas tree, the small package Mother had sent me was waiting to be opened.

The accompanying card we'd already unsealed and displayed on the mantel. I picked it up and read her heart-tugging message at the bottom: "We miss you so very much. You are in our prayers, and we are looking forward to the time we can all be together again."

The next few words brought a lump to my throat.

"Your father says to tell you that he loves you and is lonely without you here. But when your work there is done and you finally come home, he says we're *really* going to celebrate Christmas!" She'd underlined the word *really*.

My husband and the jovial student missionary arrived from another vain attempt to repair the school generator. The three of us, by candlelight, offered thanks for the best that I could manage with current provisions—an egg omelet, small boiled potatoes, a tiny tomato sliced three ways, and my newly baked cinnamon rolls.

CHRISTMAS EVE

After supper, we sat—perspiring—before the crackling fire and exchanged gifts.

I gave my husband a giant stalk of bananas and a crude wooden desktop file for organizing his school papers. Our neighbor had helped me construct it from scrap plywood. My husband gave me a charcoal-burning iron he had walked eight miles round-trip to purchase at the nearest outdoor market. Our gift to John was a small woven basket and chocolate chip cookies. His gift to us was the promise of continuing repairs on our temperamental Belgian toilet.

Trying to ignore homesickness, the three of us munched cookies and made sure the conversation stayed light. But I sure missed my mother and father and brother and sisters-in-law and nieces and aunt and uncle. I missed America!

When the conversation lapsed, my husband looked at me with a special glow in his eyes and said, "Carolyn, shall we tell Jonathan the latest news?"

I smiled self-consciously and admitted, "We're going to have a baby." Then we couldn't resist relating the response of an African acquaintance earlier in the day when we'd shared our news with him.

"Of course, you're going to have a baby," he'd countered with a condescending air. "The way your wife stood visiting so long that day in the shade of the fertility tree in your backyard . . . I knew then it was just a matter of time."

In the dancing light of our unnecessary fire, laughter died down, and lest the ensuing silence and loneliness grow too heavy, I suggested we close the evening with a reading of Luke's Christmas story. So there, beside our palm-leaf Christmas tree, far away from department-store carols and holiday lights, my husband began the ancient story of another young couple—centuries ago—who were expecting their first Child in a faraway land.

Blinking back tears of self-pity, I listened as the familiar story unfolded. For years I'd viewed the Child's coming in general terms: "God's Gift to the world." Tonight—perhaps because I was in Zaire—I heard about a Baby born in a foreign country, a tiny Missionary who gave up unspeakable comforts of His homeland to travel to a dark, underdeveloped culture and live in sinful surroundings, which were so foreign to His divine nature.

How He must have missed, as time passed, His heavenly family! He was separated from His Father for 33 years—before being killed by those He had come to serve.

I reflected on my frustration and doubts these first few months of foreign work. And now the light of Bethlehem's star showed me that any service I offered would be effective only if I sheltered *anew* the Babe in my drafty heart and allowed His spirit of *willing* and *joyful* sacrifice to become my own.

GIFT EXCHANGE

As we knelt for prayer that first Christmas Eve in Africa, my gift to the Christ Child was my heart—again—but this time more thoughtfully wrapped.

In exchange, the Holy Child's gifts to me poured down with abundance— adaptability, learning to make do with what I had, perseverance, a sense of humor, and the beginning of a nine-year love affair with God's children of another culture.

A few days later, while carefully packing away our sparse Christmas ornaments from off the mantel, I picked up the Christmas card from home and reread it.

There—in Mother's loving words—I discovered the Holy Child's greatest gift of all . . .

"Your Father says to tell you he loves you and is lonely without you here. But when your work there is done and you finally come home, he said we're really going to celebrate Christmas!"

•

Carolyn Rathbun-Sutton, editor, scriptwriter, short-story writer, and television host, writes from her home in Dayton, Tennessee.

Christmas Memories

A LOVE SONG FOR CHRISTMAS

D. T. DOIG

It had been a long, hard day in the toy department. Dominating the stuffed animal section in the big London store was Humphrey, the giant teddy bear. But even a red hat, a red muffler, and glasses hadn't been enough to give him a home.

Then, in came a tall man in glasses.

This unforgettable story by David Doig is rapidly becoming a Christmas classic.

The hands of the clock crept toward seven-thirty, and Susan Turner hoped she didn't look as tired as she felt. Her feet had become lead weights and all she could think of was the sanctuary of her apartment and the bliss of a hot bath. But there were still some late shoppers browsing about the toy department, and the sales staff at Waterson's was supposed to look cool, efficient, and cheerful, no matter what. Thank heavens tomorrow was Christmas Eve, the last day of late closing.

But as long as the day had been, the glittering scene of the toy department still held a kind of magic for Susan. Over in the realm of dolls, woolly animals, and teddy bears, the real essence of Christmas seemed to be embodied. It was old-fashioned, she knew, but it said so much more to her than the racks of boxed games and computer toys.

Standing out, foremost among them all, was Humphrey, the giant teddy bear. He sat with a red muffler around his throat and a knitted cap on his head. He wore a red heart on his chest, like a badge, and someone with inspiration had given him a pair of spectacles so that he almost looked human and wise. Or so it seemed to Susan.

Somewhere inside Susan Turner was a little girl who still would have liked to own him. He was a friend whom she greeted in the mornings, and whom she bade good night when she switched off the lights at closing time.

By eight this evening the customers had thinned out, and Susan could take a minute to sit down by her desk and take the weight off her feet.

It was during her break that she saw the tall man in glasses, moving swiftly across the department. He didn't loiter like someone looking for ideas. He walked quickly past the shelves of mechanical toys and space-age novelties, down the aisle of stuffed animals and, without hesitating, picked up Humphrey, Susan's favorite bear, and tucked him under his arm. Held horizontally with his spectacles askew, Humphrey presented a picture of outraged dignity.

"Can you help me?" the man asked, hitching Humphrey to an upright position and setting him on the desk. "I'd like to buy this guy."

"Certainly, sir." Susan collected herself swiftly, brushing aside a slight sadness at the prospect of the bear's departure. "I think Humphrey will be glad to find a home at last."

The man, who had an attractive face, became suddenly handsome when he smiled. "Humphrey? Why do you call him that?"

"It's his name," Susan told him. "It's built in." She reached over and poked the furry stomach.

"*My name is Humphrey,*" the bear declared in a rich baritone.

"There's a trapdoor with a battery in the small of his back," Susan explained. "He says his name every time you squeeze him."

The man produced his wallet and presented a credit card. "It's for a little girl of three. Do you think it's all right?"

Susan replied quite without the motivation of a saleswoman. "I think it's perfect. To a child that age, a big teddy will be almost real. He'll be a wonderful friend and I'm sure your little girl will love him."

"She's not my little girl. I'm her godfather." Then his eyes lit with new interest. "You seem to know a lot about children."

Susan felt the color rise in her cheeks. "Not really. It's just that when I was a little girl—" She paused, embarrassed. He wouldn't want to know about her early years in an orphanage, about the void in her life which had bred a longing for something that was strictly her own. She busied herself with the transaction and noted, when he signed, that his name was T. J. Grant.

"Don't bother trying to wrap him," he said. "I'll be taking him in a taxi." His eyes held hers a moment longer and she thought he was about to say more. Then the moment passed, and with a nod and a smile he was gone.

Susan sighed and wondered about T. J. Grant. She felt that in some odd manner her day had been turned upside down. It had been a long time since she'd met a man who radiated such a sense of warmth, but why should she have this sudden empty feeling as she watched him leave? Humphrey, of course, had gone too. The empty space where he had sat regarding her through his spectacles added to her sense of loss. But that, she told herself, was simply childish. She must be getting maudlin at the early age of 25.

Still, the interlude had brought nearer the end of the working day. In half an hour she'd be on her way home. Tomorrow evening she could go to a friend's home for a family gathering. She hadn't decided yet. Her friends were always thoughtful about including her at holidays. She was grateful for that, but it wasn't like having a sense of belonging to your own family.

At last it was closing time, and Susan went mechanically through the routine of checking out. Drenching rain greeted her as she let herself out of the employee's door. There was nothing to do but wait in front of the store, in the shelter of the awning, for a taxi. On a night like this it wouldn't be easy to find one.

She'd waited five minutes when a man sprinted across the street and joined her on the steps. He was carrying something bulky wrapped in a raincoat; only when he stood panting in front of her did she recognize T. J. Grant.

He was hatless and she could see raindrops glinting in his hair. "I suppose I'm too late. I was hoping to find the store still open."

Susan tried to gather her wits. "Is anything wrong?"

He lifted one end of the raincoat to reveal the placid, furry face of Humphrey. "Well, just about everything has gone wrong. I arrived here today from Brazil, all set for an old-fashioned Christmas. The idea was to surprise my old friends who'd made me their daughter's godfather. But when I called from my hotel a few minutes ago, a stranger answered the phone. My friend's subletting his apartment. His company sent him to Canada. He'll be there for at least two years. So now the question is—what do I do with this bear?"

In spite of the rain and her fatigue, Susan was amused by his helplessness, and touched. "Well," she said after a moment's thought, "you could bring him back tomorrow. Exchange him for goods of the same value, or credit."

T. J. Grant stood there, undecided, his face a little woebegone. "I suppose so," he said. "It's just—well, it's not the money. I had this good feeling about Christmas and now it's gone flat. This teddy bear—you'll think I'm mad, but now that my plans have collapsed, I feel I want to give it to some child, somebody who'd be happy to have it."

Again, Susan was touched. "There are hospitals and orphanages, if that's what you want to do. There are ways to make it a gift, but right now it's late and—"

"I'm sorry," he broke in. "It's not your problem and you must be very tired. How long have you been in that store today?"

Susan felt herself wilting again. "Twelve hours."

Now he was really contrite. "Oh, I am sorry. Look, would you—could you possibly agree to have dinner with me, right now? You must be starving and we could talk about—about Humphrey."

Susan took five seconds to make up her mind. "All right," she said. "Thank you. I'd like that." And as if to make sure her decision was irrevocable, an empty cab pulled up to the curb in front of them.

In a moment, Susan was sitting close to T. J. Grant and Humphrey, in his scarf and hat, and leaning drunkenly against the door. His spectacles had slipped down and his brown eyes seemed to regard her with a look of profound wisdom.

By the time they arrived at the restaurant, Susan knew that T. J. stood for Thomas James and that his years in Brazil had been spent helping to build a dam. The restaurant was French and Susan liked it on sight. She also liked the way Tom carried in the bear, as if it were the most natural thing in the world.

The head waiter smiled a welcome, apparently unmoved by the presence of Humphrey. Yes, there was a table for three, he said.

The dining room was three-quarters full, and when Humphrey was safely seated, heads began to turn in their direction.

"It's a true-life case of beauty and the beast," Tom said. "They can't help looking."

Susan grimaced. "Maybe so, but I wonder which of us looks more like the beast."

"You look beautiful," Tom said.

As the coffee and the excellent food began to restore Susan's strength and morale, she felt the strain of the long day vanish. And the longer she sat opposite T. J. Grant, the more pleased she was that it had all happened.

"About Humphrey," she said at last. "It's a little late to find a home for him tonight. But there's a children's hospital nearby. I'm sure they'd be glad to accept him. He would be ideal for the permanent toy nursery which is in use all the time."

Tom considered this. "So he wouldn't actually belong to someone?"

"Probably not. The children will be getting plenty of toys from their relatives and friends. But Humphrey—well, you would need to know some child personally to give him as a present, the way you want to."

"I see." Tom paused in thought while the waiter refilled their cups.

On an impulse, Susan told Tom about her childhood. "I grew up in an orphanage," she said. "And we had toys, of course, but I always wanted a big teddy bear. It never happened and I suppose that's why I'm still a bit sentimental about them."

A soberness crossed Tom's face, like the shadow of something far distant. "I really don't know much about children," he said. "I only had one for two years."

Susan's eyes widened and her spirits took a surprising plunge. "You're married then?"

"I was," he said. "Several years ago. It was before I began looking for jobs in odd corners of the world. My wife and daughter were killed in a car accident."

In a flash Susan felt she understood the complexity of this man's character. Beneath the armor of everyday life lay the hunger, the loss, and the instinct to make a child happy, some real and tangible child, although it was not his own.

As life so often does, the next moment brought them both back to coping with absurdities. The waiter, nearing their table to refill their coffee cups, caught his foot, somehow, and stumbled into Humphrey's chair, knocking the bear to the floor.

Heads turned once more to their table. From below, activated by the impact, came the baritone of the bear's total vocabulary. *"My name is Humphrey."*

A ripple of laughter went through the restaurant. Humphrey was rescued, the waiter reassured, and a few minutes later Susan and Tom were out on the street again.

"That was fun," Susan said. "I'll always remember this evening." It had stopped raining and the city lights glistened on the wet pavement.

"Does it have to end here?" Tom asked. "It's early yet. Maybe we could find a good movie."

For Susan the past two hours had banished weariness and brought a vitality she had not felt for a long time. The prospect of prolonging this one pleasant evening was too strong to resist.

And so it was that they arrived, complete with bear, at the theater box office. A bored girl slid three tickets toward Tom, without raising an eyebrow at the bear.

The movie was good; a romantic thriller. During the engrossing scene, with the suspense slowly mounting, Humphrey began to topple forward, his head approaching the shoulder of the man in the seat in front.

Tom shot out a hand and caught the bear just in time—by the stomach. For one awful fraction of a second, Tom realized nothing could stop the result. The small recording inside the bear went relentlessly into action. *"My name is Humphrey."*

The nearby section of the audience were jerked out of their enthrallment by the penetrating voice of the bear. One of these growling interruptions might have been only a mild distraction, but, to Susan and Tom's horror, the sound track kept repeating.

"My name is Humphrey. My name is Humphrey. My name is Humphrey."

Amid indignant protests, Tom grabbed Susan's arm with one hand, Humphrey's with the other. "Let's get out of here—fast!"

As they squeezed their way down the row and up the aisle to the exit, Tom muffled Humphrey's voice in the folds of his raincoat. Out on the street, they dissolved into helpless laughter.

Susan opened the flap in Humphrey's back and removed the battery. "I think he's done enough talking for tonight."

Tom aimed a right hook at Humphrey's innocent face. "He's certainly given you a hard day. I'm afraid I've been a nuisance myself."

Susan handed him the now silent bear. "I wouldn't have missed it for anything."

Another taxi took them to the entrance of Susan's apartment. When Tom got out and stood with her on the sidewalk, she was aware that something was about to end that she would find hard to forget. This chance meeting with T. J. Grant, this casual but memorable evening had now reached its inevitable conclusion.

"Well, good luck finding a home for Humphrey," she said. "I suppose you'll be moving on somewhere."

"Nowhere to move to," he replied. "No family now, and all I have in this town is a bank account, a lawyer, and a desk in my firm's head office. But right now, all I need is sleep."

She saw with concern that his face was pale and behind his glasses his eyes were heavy with fatigue. It suddenly hit her that only this morning he had flown in from South America. A wave of sadness brought a tightness to her throat. "Good-bye, then. Perhaps you'll let me know what happens to Humphrey."

Barely 10 minutes later, she was preparing a hot drink when the sound of the doorbell made her start with surprise. When she opened the door, there was T. J. Grant, holding the bear.

By now she was getting used to the unexpected. Without losing her poise, she said calmly, "Come in and have some coffee. I'm just making it."

He stood inside the door. "I had to come back," he said. "I stopped the cab because something suddenly dawned on me. I know now who I want to give Humphrey to. He's yours, Susan. After this evening, I couldn't give him to anyone else."

Susan's heart began to thump wildly. She put Humphrey down tenderly in the nearest chair, but it was some seconds before she was able to speak. "I'd love to have him. But if I do take him, he'll always be partly yours."

Tom came and stood beside her. It seemed natural that he take her hand. "If I have a share in Humphrey, could that include a share in you?"

For Susan, the room, previously empty and lifeless, appeared to sparkle and come alive. "Well, for a start, come here tomorrow when you've had enough sleep. We'll celebrate Humphrey's homecoming. How about that?"

Tom gave a sigh of relief. "I've been wondering if I could survive Christmas in a strange hotel. But Humphrey has solved everything."

He punched the bear's midriff, but this time Humphrey said nothing. He only stared ahead with his soft brown eyes and seemed to smile secretly.

•

David Doig (1911–1990) was a native of the Isle of Skye in Scotland and died there in 1990. He was an extremely prolific writer, and his stories have been published all over the world.

Christmas Memories

CHRISTMAS, LOST AND FOUND

SHIRLEY BARKSDALE

It was not a good Christmas that year. Their Christmas boy had come to them at Christmas—and left them at Christmas.

And they? "Without his invincible yuletide spirit, we were like poorly trained dancers, unable to perform after the music had stopped."

So they fled. Now, sixteen long years later, they'd returned—but really had no idea why.

Ever since being featured in *McCall's* and *Reader's Digest*, this story has been percolating its way into the hearts of thousands of readers.

We called him our Christmas Boy because he came to us during that season of joy, when he was just six days old. Already his eyes twinkled more brightly than the lights on his first tree.

Later, as our family expanded, he made it clear that only he had the expertise to select and decorate the tree each year. He rushed the season, starting his gift list before we'd even finished the Thanksgiving turkey. He pressed us into singing carols, our croaky voices sounding more froglike than ever compared to his perfect pitch. He stirred us up, led us through a round of merry chaos.

Then, on his 24th Christmas, he left us as unexpectedly as he had come. A car accident, on an icy Denver street, on his way home to his young wife and infant daughter. But first he had stopped by the family home to decorate our tree, a ritual he had never abandoned.

Without his invincible yuletide spirit, we were like poorly trained dancers, unable to perform after the music had stopped. In our grief, his father and I sold our home, where memories clung to every room. We moved to California, leaving behind our support system of friends and church. All the wrong moves.

It seemed I had come full circle, back to those early years when there had been just my parents and me. Christmas had always been a quiet, hurried affair, unlike the celebrations at my friends' homes, which were lively and peopled with rollicking relatives. I vowed then that someday I'd marry and have six children, and that at Christmas my house would vibrate with energy and love.

I found the man who shared my dream, but we had not reckoned on the surprise of infertility. Undaunted, we applied for adoption, ignoring gloomy prophecies that an adopted child would not be the same as "our own flesh and blood." Even then, hope did not run high; the waiting list was long. But against all odds, within a year he arrived and was ours. Then nature surprised us again, and in rapid succession we added two biological children to the family. Not as many as we had hoped for, but compared to my quiet childhood, three made an entirely satisfactory crowd.

Those friends were right about adopted children not being the same. He wasn't the least like the rest of us. Through his own unique heredity, he brought color into our lives with his gift of music, his irrepressible good cheer, his bossy wit. He made us look and behave better than we were.

In the 16 years that followed his death, time added chapters to our lives. His widow remarried and had a son; his daughter graduated from high school. His brother married and began his own Christmas traditions in another state. His sister, an artist, seemed fulfilled by her career. His father and I grew old enough to retire, and in December of 1987 we decided to return to Denver. The call home was unclear; we knew only that we yearned for some indefinable connection, for something lost that had to be retrieved before time ran out.

We slid into Denver on the tail end of a blizzard. Blocked highways forced us through the city, past the Civic Center, ablaze with thousands of lights—a scene I was not ready to face. This same trek had been one of our Christmas Boy's favorite holiday traditions. He had been relentless in his insistence that we all pile into the car, its windows fogged over with our warm breath, its tires fighting for a grip in ice.

I looked away from the lights and fixed my gaze on the distant Rockies, where he had loved to go barreling up the mountainside in search of the perfect tree. Now in the foothills there was his grave—a grave I could not bear to visit.

Once we were settled in the small, boxy house, so different from the family home where we had orchestrated our lives, we hunkered down like two barn swallows who had missed the last migration south. While I stood staring toward the snowcapped mountains one day, I heard the sudden screech of car brakes, then the impatient peal of the doorbell. There stood our granddaughter, and in the gray-green eyes and impudent grin I saw the reflection of our Christmas Boy.

Behind her, lugging a large pine tree, came her mother, stepfather and nine-year-old half brother. They swept past us in a flurry of laughter; they uncorked the sparkling cider and toasted our homecoming. Then they decorated the tree and piled gaily wrapped packages under the boughs.

"You'll recognize the ornaments," said my former daughter-in-law. "They were his. I saved them for you."

"I picked out most of the gifts, Grandma," said the nine-year-old, whom I hardly knew.

When I murmured, in remembered pain, that we hadn't had a tree for, well, 16 years, our cheeky granddaughter said, "Then it's time to shape up!"

They left in a whirl, shoving one another out the door, but not before asking us to join them the next morning for church, then dinner at their home.

"Oh, we just can't," I began.

"You sure can," ordered our granddaughter, as bossy as her father had been. "I'm singing the solo, and I want to see you there."

"Bring earplugs," advised the nine-year-old.

We had long ago given up the poignant Christmas services, but now, under pressure, we sat rigid in the front pew, fighting back tears.

Then it was solo time. Our granddaughter swished (her father would have swaggered) to center stage, and the magnificent voice soared, clear and true, in perfect pitch. She sang "O Holy Night," which brought back bittersweet memories. In a rare emotional response, the congregation applauded in delight. How her father would have relished that moment.

We had been alerted that there would be a "whole mess of people" for dinner— but 35? Assorted relatives filled every corner of the house; small children, noisy and exuberant, seemed to bounce off the walls. I could not sort out who belonged to whom, but it didn't matter. They all belonged to one another. They took us in, enfolded us in joyous camaraderie. We sang carols in loud, off-key voices, saved only by that amazing soprano.

Sometime after dinner, before the winter sunset, it occurred to me that a true family is not always one's own flesh and blood. It is a climate of the heart. Had it not been for our adopted son, we would not now be surrounded by caring strangers who would help us to hear the music again.

Later, not yet ready to give up the day, our granddaughter asked us to come along with her. "I'll drive," she said. "There's a place I like to go." She humped behind the wheel of the car and, with the confidence of a newly licensed driver, zoomed off toward the foothills.

Alongside the headstone rested a small, heart-shaped rock, slightly cracked, painted by our artist daughter. On its weathered surface she had written: "To my brother, with love." Across the crest of the grave lay a holly-bright Christmas wreath. Our number-two son admitted, when asked, that he sent one every year.

In the chilly but somehow comforting silence, we were not prepared for our unpredictable granddaughter's next move. Once more that day her voice, so like her father's, lifted in song, and the mountainside echoed the chorus of "Joy to the World," on and on into infinity.

When the last pure note had faded, I felt, for the first time since our son's death, a sense of peace, of the positive continuity of life, of renewed faith and hope. The real meaning of Christmas had been restored to us. Hallelujah!

•

Short-story writer **Shirley Barksdale** currently writes from her home in Highlands Ranch, Colorado.

THE GOOD THINGS IN LIFE

ARTHUR GORDON

They were coming back this Christmas morning, coming back to where it had all started. Since that time, growing fame had come to him—changed him, warped him. Self had pushed God aside. Mary wondered: *Will it work? Will the little church be on my side?*

Near the crest of the hill he felt the rear wheels of the car spin for half a second, and he felt a flash of the unreasonable irritability that had been plaguing him lately. He said, a bit grimly, "Good thing it didn't snow more than an inch or two. We'd be in trouble if it had."

His wife was driving. She often did, so that he could make notes for a sermon or catch up on his endless correspondence by dictating into the tape recorder he had had built into the car. Now she looked out at the woods and fields gleaming in the morning sunlight. "It's pretty, though. And Christmasy. We haven't had a white Christmas like this in years."

He gave her an amused and affectionate glance. "You always see the best side of things, don't you, my love?"

"Well, after hearing you urge umpteen congregations to do precisely that . . ."

Arnold Barclay smiled, and some of the lines of tension and fatigue went out of his face. "Remember the bargain we made twenty years ago? I'd do the preaching and you'd do the practicing."

Her mouth curved faintly. "I remember."

They came to a crossroads, and he found that after all these years he still remembered the sign: LITTLEFIELD, 1 MILE. He said, "How's the time?"

She glanced at the diamond watch on her wrist: his present to her this year. "A little after ten."

He leaned forward and switched on the radio. In a moment his own voice, strong and resonant, filled the car, preaching a Christmas sermon prepared and recorded weeks before. He listened to a sentence or two, then smiled sheepishly and turned it off. "Just wanted to hear how I sounded."

"You sound fine," Mary Barclay said. "You always do."

They passed a farmhouse, the new snow sparkling like diamonds on the roof, the Christmas wreath gay against the front door. "Who lived there?" he asked. "Peterson, wasn't it? No, Johannsen."

"That's right," his wife said. "Eric Johannsen. Remember the night he made you hold the lantern while the calf was born?"

"Do I ever!" He rubbed his forehead wearily. "About this new television proposition, Mary. What do you think? It would be an extra load, I know. But I'd be reaching an enormous audience. The biggest—"

She put her hand on his arm. "Darling, it's Christmas Day. Can't we talk about it later?"

"Why, sure," he said, but something in him was offended all the same. The television proposal was important. Why, in fifteen minutes he would reach ten times as many people as Saint Paul had reached in a lifetime! He said, "How many people did the Littlefield church hold, Mary? About a hundred, wasn't it?"

"Ninety-six," his wife said. "To be exact."

"Ninety-six!" He gave a rueful laugh. "Quite a change of pace."

It was that, all right. It was years since he had preached in anything but metropolitan churches. The Littlefield parish had been the beginning. Now, on Christmas morning, he was going back. Back for an hour or two, to stand in the little pulpit where he had preached his first hesitant, fumbling sermon twenty years ago.

He let his head fall back against the seat and closed his eyes. The decision to go back had not been his, really; it had been Mary's. She handled all his appointments, screening the innumerable invitations to preach or speak. A month ago she had come to him. There was a request, she said, for him to go back to Littlefield and preach a sermon on Christmas morning.

"Littlefield?" he had said, incredulous. "What about that Washington invitation?" He had been asked to preach to a congregation that would, he knew, include senators and cabinet members.

"We haven't answered it yet," she said. "We could drive to Littlefield on Christmas morning, if we got up early enough . . ."

He had stared at her. "You mean, you think we ought to go back there?"

She had looked back at him calmly. "That's up to you, Arnold." But he knew what she wanted him to say.

Making such a decision wasn't so hard at the moment, he thought wearily. Not resenting afterward—that was the difficult part. Maybe it wouldn't be so bad. The church would be horribly overcrowded, the congregation would be mostly farmers, but . . .

The car stopped; he opened his eyes.

They were at the church, all right. There it sat by the side of the road, just as it always had—if anything, it looked smaller than he remembered it. Around it the fields stretched away, white and unbroken, to the neighboring farmhouses. But there were no cars, there was no crowd, there was no sign of anyone. The church was shuttered and silent.

He looked at Mary, bewildered. She did not seem surprised. She pushed open the car door. "Let's go inside, shall we? I still have a key."

The church was cold. Standing in the icy gloom, he could see his breath steam in the gray light. He said, and his voice sounded strange, "Where is everybody? You said there was a request . . ."

"There was a request," Mary said. "From me." She moved forward slowly until she was standing by the pulpit. "Arnold," she said, "the finest sermon I ever heard you preach was right here in this church. It was your first Christmas sermon; we hadn't been married long. You didn't know our first baby was on the way—but I did. Maybe that's why I remember so well what you said.

"You said that God had tried every way possible to get through to people. He tried prophets and miracles and revelations—and nothing worked. So then He said, "I'll send them something they can't fail to understand. 'I'll send them the simplest and yet the most wonderful thing in all My creation. I'll send them a Baby . . .' Do you remember that?"

He nodded wordlessly.

"Well," she said, "I heard that they had no minister here now, so I knew they wouldn't be having a service this morning. And I thought . . . well, I thought it might be good for . . . for both of us if you could preach that sermon again. Right here, where your ministry began. I just thought . . ."

Her voice trailed off, but he knew what she meant. He knew what she was trying to tell him, although she was too loyal and too kind to say it in words. That he had gotten away from the sources of his strength. That as success had come to him, as his reputation had grown larger, some things in him had grown smaller. The selflessness. The humility. The most important things of all.

He stood there, silent, seeing himself with a terrifying clarity: the pride, the ambition, the hunger for larger and larger audiences. Not for the glory of God. For the glory of Arnold Barclay.

He clenched his fists, feeling panic grip him, a sense of terror and guilt unlike anything he had ever known. Then faintly, underneath the panic, something else stirred. He glanced around the little church. She was right, Mary was right, and perhaps it wasn't too late. Perhaps here, now, he could rededicate himself . . .

Abruptly he stripped off his overcoat, tossed it across the back of a pew. He reached out and took both of Mary's hands. He heard himself laugh, an eager, boyish laugh. "We'll do it! We'll do it just the way we used to! You open the shutters; that was your job, remember? I'll start the furnace. We'll have a Christmas service just for the two of us. I'll preach that sermon, all for you!"

She turned quickly to the nearest window, raised it, began fumbling with the catch that held the shutters. He opened the door that led to the cellar steps. Down in the frigid basement he found the furnace squatting, as black and malevolent as ever. He flung open the iron door. No fire was laid, but along the wall wood was stacked, and kindling, and newspapers.

He began to crumple papers and thrust them into the furnace, heedless of the soot that blackened his fingers. Overhead he heard the sound that made him pause. Mary was trying the wheezy old melodeon. "Ring the bell, too," he shouted up the stairs. "We might as well do the job right!"

He heard her laugh. A moment later, high in the belfry, the bell began to ring. Its tone was as clear and resonant as ever, and the sound brought back a flood of memories: the baptisms, the burials, the Sunday dinners at the old farmhouses, the honesty and brusqueness and simple goodness of the people.

He stood there, listening, until the bell was silent. Then he struck a match and held it to the newspapers. Smoke curled reluctantly. He reached up, adjusted the old damper, tried again. This time a tongue of flame flickered. For perhaps five minutes he watched it, hovering over it, blowing on it. When he was sure that it was kindled, he went back up the cellar steps.

The church was a blaze of sunlight. Where the window glass was clear, millions of dust motes whirled and danced; where there were panes of stained glass, the rays fell on the old floor in pools of ruby and topaz and amethyst. Mary was standing at the church door. "Arnold," she said, "come here."

He went and stood beside her. After the darkness of the cellar, the sun on the snow was so bright that he couldn't see anything.

"Look," she said in a whisper. "They're coming."

Cupping his hands round his eyes, he stared out across the glistening whiteness, and he saw that she was right. They were coming. Across the fields. Down the roads. Some on foot. Some in cars. They were coming, he knew, not to hear him, not to hear any preacher, however great. They were coming because it was Christmas Day, and this was their church and its bell was calling them. They were coming because they wanted someone to give them the ancient message, to tell them the good news.

He stood there with his arm round his wife's shoulders and the soot black on his face and the overflowing happiness in his heart. "Merry Christmas," he said. "Merry Christmas. And thank you. Thank you, darling."

•

During his long career, **Arthur Gordon** (1912–2002) edited such magazines as *Cosmopolitan, Good Housekeeping,* and *Guideposts.* He was author of a number of books as well as hundreds of short stories.

Christmas Memories

O LITTLE FLOCK

TEMPLE BAILEY

Her husband, who had always been her mainstay, was dead. Her money was almost gone, and her two oldest children insisted that she spend it all for Christmas. So what was she to do when all the bills came in?

Then Dr. Wade—who had loved her "for a thousand years"—stepped in.

The choir was practicing Christmas carols in the church next door. There are some advantages in living next to a church, even if you are in a shabby old apartment house which backs up to the sacred edifice, with a frontage on an unfashionable thoroughfare.

One advantage, Sara had found was on moonlight nights, when you could look out upon the high, delicate spire etched against the golden sky, and be flooded with a sense of the world's beauty. And another was when, in moments of deep depression, the sound of the organ swept over you in waves of celestial harmony.

At times, however, Sara felt there were no advantages. As tonight when the reiteration of the Christmas carols got on her nerves.

"It is all very well," was her mental challenge, "to sing like that. As if Christmas Day made up for everything. But it doesn't. Not when you have four children. Not when every one of them wants something you can't give. Not when you haven't any money. Not when you don't dare face your bills. Not when—"

She stopped there. Why go on, with that crash of exultation weakening her protests?

"Oh, take the gift,
In joy receive;
All things are his
Who will believe;
O Little Flock,
What words can tell,
The bliss of souls—"

It was really a beautiful carol, but Sara had no patience with it. "If they knew anything about sheep, they wouldn't talk of flocks."

Sara knew a great deal about sheep. Her girlhood had been spent on her grandfather's old place in Virginia. His sheep had roamed the hills of Albemarle, picturesque at long distance, but not so meek as the poets have them. Sara had once owned a pet lamb, which had shown revolutionary traits. When she wanted it to follow, it had had a way of kicking up its heels and ramping sideways down the road, leaving her dismayed and disconcerted.

And now her own little flock had kicked up its heels. And she didn't know what to do about it. She didn't know what to do about anything. If only the children knew how helpless she felt without their father.

But of course they couldn't know. They were young, and youth is thoughtless. She must seem to her children quite mature and self-sufficient. They couldn't know the panic in her heart when she thought of the years ahead of her.

She had made her Christmas plans with certainty that they would cooperate. She had felt sure that the older ones, at least, would share her sense of responsibility when the situation was explained to them.

So that very night at dinner she had said, "My darlings, some of Daddy's investments have gone wrong. I'm afraid we shall have to have a rather shabby Christmas."

"What do you mean by 'shabby'?" young Randolf, in his father's place at the head of the table, had flung out.

"Oh, well, I wondered if we couldn't go down to Solomon's Shore for the holidays. We'd be very cozy and happy and—"

They stopped her with a chorus: "Solomon's Shore!"

No mistaking that tone of horrified protest. She tried to ignore it: "We could have the time of our lives, couldn't we?"

"We could *not*," this from Kathleen, seventeen and a beauty, "and anyhow there's my Christmas Eve party."

"My dear, I'm afraid you'll have to give that up."

"Do you mean," there was a sort of breathlessness about Kathleen, "that I am not to entertain my friends, after I've been asked *everywhere*—asked and asked and asked, and *never* paid back?"

Sara, white and troubled, demanded, "What can I do?"

Then young Randolf, cocksurely, "Kits is right, Mother. She ought to have her party, even if we have to sell the family jewels."

"But we haven't any jewels, Randy."

"Don't be so literal-minded, Mums. What I mean is, let's forget dull care at Christmastime and mortgage the house and lot."

"But we haven't any house and lot," she answered patiently.

"There you go again. It's this way. Cut out economy during the holidays, and give us a whale of a time, and we'll live on bread and cheese if we have to. Kits and I have social obligations, and they've got to be met. We want a party and clothes for it."

"Randy, I can't pay my January bills."

"Pay your February ones, then. Lots of people let them run over, and we'll take lean pickings for a month or two."

She tried to tell them it was impossible. But they bore down with their arguments until she had no strength left to combat them. Yet it was not their arguments which finally weakened her, but Kathleen's lovely face rainwashed by tears. "We'd be *buried* at Solomon's Shore, Mother. What made you think of it?"

"Your daddy and I loved it," said Sara simply, "and so did you when you were little."

"Oh, well, of course; but things are different in these days," said young Randolph toploftically. "We have to keep up with the procession."

Arguments, arguments, arguments! At last Sara told them desperately, "I'll see what I can do. I have to think of our future."

"You think too much," her son promptly assured her; "just gather your rosebuds, old dear, and forget tomorrow."

After which helpful remark, he got up from the table, and later went off with Kathleen and some young friends to the movies, leaving Sara high and dry, as it were, on the shores of her dilemma.

After their departure, Mary Virginia, who was eight and had some lessons to do before she went to bed, looked up from her place under the lamp and said, "I think it would be dreadful if Kits couldn't."

And Bobs, the baby, being tucked in, added a codicil to his usual prayers, "Please, God, give Kits her Christmas party."

Was it any wonder that Sara, standing now by the window, listening to that triumphant choir, flung a challenge to their glorious tidings? Christmas was not a time of peace and good will. It was a time of spending more than you could afford. It was a time of trying to keep up with other people. It was a time not of light-heartedness, but of heaviness. Yet the children were young. And youth had a right to good times and gaiety.

Having a Liberty Bond or two, Sara sold them. She sold them in order that Kits might have her party and Randy his first dress clothes. Kathleen, flaming into more-than-ever loveliness, said, "Oh, Mother, you're a darling," and Randy patted her on the back and called her a good sport.

Well, of course it was something to be approved by your children. Sara told herself with a touch of sarcasm that mothers had stolen for less. She was amazed to find herself appreciating the satire of the situation. Having had their own way, Randy and Kathleen proceeded to show their mother they adored her for letting them have it. They led her on into further extravagances. Kits' party, they said, must be the real thing. No homemade sandwiches and salads. Old Martha, their cook, might do for every day, but not for this occasion. A caterer must do it all. "We might as well be killed for a sheep as a lamb," Randy proclaimed grandiloquently.

Being again reminded of flocks and fleece, Sara wanted to retort that you couldn't eat your mutton and have it too. But she refrained. She knew the futility of attempting to stem the tide of Randy's disputations.

She was, however, not happy. She was oppressed by a sense of her lack of proper guardianship. What if they were wrecked on the shoals of debt? Who would save them? And wouldn't it be her fault if they went under?

She lay awake nights thinking about it. At last she showed dark circles under her eyes, an unwonted paleness.

One morning, coming to the breakfast table with a blinding headache, she seemed so worn and spent that Randy asked solicitously, "Aren't you well?"

"Yes. Why?"

"You don't look it. You'd better see Wade Phillips."

But Sara didn't want to see Wade. She knew he would say at once, "It's those darned children. They're draining the life out of you."

Wade had been a friend and college chum of her husband, and was the family doctor. He was also Sara's adviser and friend. He didn't approve of Sara's attitude toward her children. "You're too good to them," he told her, "and they take advantage of it. They'd be a lot better off if you'd treat 'em rough."

She flamed, "I want them to love me."

"They'll love you more if you don't let them impose on you. You've got to show them that you're the head of the house."

He embroidered this theme somewhat, one night when he came to look at Mary Virginia's tonsils. "Parents," he remarked with a spoon in Mary Virginia's throat, "ought to be mid-Victorian."

Mary Virginia, regaining presently the use of her tongue, demanded, "What's mid-Victorian?"

"Well, those were the days when little children had to mind their mothers."

"I do mind her."

"You didn't when you wouldn't wear your overshoes, and got your feet wet. And now Mother has to nurse you. If you and Bobby and Kits and Randy were mine I'd shut you up in cages."

Mary Virginia was entranced. "*Would* you?"

"Yes. And it wouldn't be as nice as you think," he replied, adding, "And if you get your feet wet again I'll cut out your tonsils."

With that he left her and went downstairs with Sara. "What have you been doing to yourself?" he asked, as they stood in front of the fire.

"Why?"

"You look as if a puff of wind would blow you away."

"I'm a little tired, that's all."

"I'll bet those darned offspring of yours are acting up."

"I wish you wouldn't call them names. If they are troublesome it's my fault."

"Nonsense; I'd manage them."

"You *do* manage them," she said, "and the more you bully them the more they adore you."

He laughed a little, but his eyes had a softened look. "I only bully them," he said, "when I have a just cause. And they know it."

In the moment's silence which followed, the voices of the choir broke in:

"*I saw three ships come sailing by,*
  Sailing by, sailing by,

I saw three ships come sailing by
On Christmas Day in the morning!"

That's a dandy old carol," Wade remarked, "about ships and things. Sara, I sometimes feel that I made a mistake when I studied medicine. I'd like to be a pirate and pick you up under my arm and carry you off to unknown seas. It wouldn't hurt the children to know what it would mean to be without a mother."

When Randy's new clothes were delivered, he tried them on and displayed himself to the assembled family. "Can you beat that?" he inquired modestly. "You've some looker for a son, Mumsie."

He was rather splendid, Sara told herself, with his thin grace, the fresh bloom on his cheeks, his crisp blond hair, his air of taking the world as he wanted it.

"Dance with me, Kits," he commanded, and as the two beautiful young creatures stepped in time to the music of the phonograph, Sara's heart leaped high in her breast. They were her own and they loved her.

Yet in the darkness of the night she would sometimes ask herself, *What is love worth if it makes no sacrifices? If I should set myself against them—what then?*

Now and then she tried feebly to oppose her will to theirs, as when Kathleen, whose new dress for the party was a clear and lovely red, declared that she must have a fan to match it. "A big one. All the girls are getting them."

"Dearest, I can't afford another thing."

"You might call it my Christmas present."

"The party is my present to you, Kits."

"Mother, Uncle Wade always gives me something. Couldn't you hint to him?"

"Kathleen!"

"I don't see why you take that tone about it. And I might as well have a fan as some of those awful things men always pick out—books or work-baskets,"

As it happened, Wade dropped in that very afternoon for a cup of tea. "I've been thinking," he said, over the buttered muffins, "of giving Kathleen a set of books. What would she like? There's a new edition of Stevenson."

Sara poured him a fresh cup of tea before she answered. She put in three lumps of sugar and more cream than was good for him.

Then she said casually, "Do you know—I think she'd rather have something—silly."

"Silly?"

"Feminine, I mean. Like a—fan."

"Great guns! How am I going to choose it?"

She passed the plate of buttered muffins. "Would you like me to help you?"

"I would. When? Tomorrow afternoon?"

Well, they bought the fan. A beautiful thing, all waving plumes, flamingo-tinted. It was extravagantly expensive. "Oh, Wade," Sara protested when she learned the price, "you mustn't pay so much."

"Why not? Don't you like it?"

"It's lovely, of course."

"Well, then."

But Sara felt it was not well, it was ill. The cost of the fan would have fed her and the children for a week. They couldn't keep this up. Kits *couldn't* go on having everything she wanted. They would have to stop.

At last arrived a crisis: "Mother, you can't wear that dress."

Kathleen had come home one afternoon and found her mother putting some extra touches on an old black lace. "You simply can't," she repeated.

"Why not?"

"It's so utterly out of style. And it makes you look years older."

"I have spent all the money I can possibly afford, Kathleen."

"But it will be only fifty dollars more. I saw a dress in the window—blue chiffon with silver. You'd look stunning in it, Mother."

Randy arriving in the midst of the discussion, contributed another of his helpful remarks: "You really ought to have it. Can't you dig down in the treasure chest and find some pieces of eight?"

She told him firmly that she couldn't and wouldn't. She didn't dare think of her treasure chest, otherwise known as her safe-deposit box. The few bonds she had kept there as an anchor to windward were gone. All except for fifty dollars.

It would buy the dress. But it shouldn't. Her mind was made up. She mustn't spend another cent for nonessentials.

But Kathleen didn't look on the new gown as a nonessential. "I should think, you'd want us to be proud of you. I should think you'd want to look your best. I should think you wouldn't want us to be—ashamed of you, Mother."

Surely the child couldn't know how those words had stabbed.

That night Wade Phillips asked Sara to go to one of the new plays with him.

Sara wore the old black lace.

"You're beautiful tonight," Wade said.

Her hands lay in her lap. They were lovely hands, slender and aristocratic. "You should have had the fan," Wade said, "only it should be blue to match your eyes."

Sara's hurt heart was comforted. At least Wade wasn't ashamed of her.

After the play they had supper at one of the best hotels. Wade ordered lobster meat under glass with mushrooms and a creamed paprika sauce, a crisp salad and, at the end, little cups of coffee. It was all delicious and Sara enjoyed it, until Wade spoke about the Christmas party. "I'm coming if I can. And I want all of your dances."

"I'm not going to dance."

"Why not?"

"I'm going to keep in the background."

"Why?"

Before she knew it she was telling him. Never before had she complained to him of the children. But now it all came out. That she had fought against having the party. That she had yielded at last against her better judgment, that to pay for it and the attendant expenses she had sold her bonds and mortgaged her income many months ahead. And that now at the very end, when she had refused to go on to other extravagances, they had said dreadful things to her.

All the time she was telling him, in the back of her mind was a sense of utter disloyalty to the family code, which had hitherto sealed her lips to outsiders, yet she wanted sympathy and expected it when she finished her story.

Wade wasted no breath in saying he was sorry for her. "Do you mean," he demanded, "that you've let them spend all that money?"

"What could I do, Wade? I wanted them to be happy."

"You could have told them to wake up and march shoulder to shoulder with you."

"I did. I tried to make them see, but they wouldn't, and now this last thing—"

She had not intended to tell him about the dress, but she did. That they wanted her to buy it with her last fifty dollars.

He gave an attentive ear: "What kind of dress?"

"Blue chiffon."

He asked a question or two after that. Where had she seen it? And what advantage it would have over the black lace? "You can't look lovelier than you do tonight, Sara. Where are their eyes?"

Going home he made up for any seeming lack of sympathy. Indeed Sara was a bit alarmed at the trend of the things he said to her. Once he laid his hand over hers, the big kind hand that had helped her over so many rough places. "You need somebody to take care of you."

In the morning early, Mary Virginia came and got into Sara's bed. "Mother," she demanded, "aren't we going to have a tree?"

"Darling, we can't. We've spent all of our money for Kit's party."

Mary Virginia's voice had a disconsolate sound: "I didn't think we could have Christmas without a tree."

"Just this once, darling. Next year we'll have our tree at Solomon's Shore the way we had when you were little."

"Tell me about it."

"Me, too," said Bobby, who had arrived on the scene.

The two of them snuggled down beside their mother, rosy and bright-eyed with anticipation. "Tell us."

"Well, then, there is always snow on Solomon's Shore, so that the world is white down to the very edge of the water, and then it is blue where the waves stretch out till they meet the sky."

"Ad the sky is blue like sapphires," chanted Mary Virginia, who had heard all this before and who loved it.

"Yes. And all along the bluff above the blue sea and the blue sky are the tall spruces—"

"That stand like sentinels."

"Yes. And in between the tall trees are the little ones—"

"Just waiting to be cut for Christmas."

"Yes. And on the day before Christmas we would all go out with Daddy, and he would cut down a little tree, and we would drag it through the snow to the house and set it up by the big fireplace, and then when we were all asleep—"

"Santa Claus would come and trim it!"

"And then the very first thing in the morning we would go out and look at the Christmas star."

"Twistmas 'tar," chortled Bobby.

Mary Virginia turned on him. "You didn't see it, Bobby. You weren't there."

"Where were I?"

"Up in heaven with the stars," said the orthodox Mary Virginia.

Sara, ignoring this interlude, went on with her story: "Then we would sing 'O little town!'"

"Let's sing it now," said Mary Virginia.

So the three of them sang it; Sara, with her soft brown braids and parted hair making a Madonna of herself; Bobby, gold-crowned like his father; and Mary Virginia, lusty follower of the faith.

And while they sang, Sara's thoughts went back to the daddy with the gold crown, and to the still white mornings down there by the sea.

"Mother," said Mary Virginia, stopping in the midst of a verse, "what are you crying about?"

"I was thinking of Daddy."

"Well, I like to think about him. It doesn't make me cry."

There was about Mary Virginia a stimulating quality. Sara felt that some day she was going to lean, not on Randy or Kathleen, but on this little daughter who already began to show something of her father's strength.

Bobby demanded, "Tell some more."

"Well, we went in and had breakfast and there was the tree with popcorn on it and nuts—"

"And shiny red apples and tiny wax candles."

"Yes. And after we had had our presents, old Martha popped the turkey into the oven and we went for a walk, and when we came back—"

"We ate it all up!" They fell on her and hugged her.

Having subsided presently Mary Virginia said: "Oh, Mother, can't we?"

"Can't you *what*?"

"Go down this year?"

"My dear, I thought you wanted Kits to have her party."

Mary Virginia had a just mind. "Well," she admitted, "I did. But I don't."

"Why not?"

"It doesn't seem like Christmas."

It didn't seem like Christmas. And it didn't seem fair to the younger children.

Sara thought about it all that day. Tomorrow was Christmas Eve, and already the house was in the process of being prepared for the party. Sara and old Martha had more than they could do. Kathleen for once proved equal to the emergency. She dusted and decorated for dear life.

It was when everything was spick and span, and Sara was resting from her labors, that Kathleen brought in a big box.

"Oh, Mumsie, you bought it!" she cried ecstatically.

"Bought what?"

"The dress. I opened it downstairs." She dropped the box to embrace her mother. "You darling sport, to get everything from fan to slippers."

"Fan to slippers!" Sara repeated mechanically.

Kathleen was flinging tissue paper out of the box. "You'll be a dream, dearest." She rushed into the hall and called over the stair rail, "Randy, come up ands see Mother's darling dress." He came and found his mother staring down at the chiffon gown of heavenly blue, the fan to match, the slippers.

She lifted dazed eyes. "But I didn't buy it."

"Then who?"

Sara knew. Wade had done it!

Kathleen was searching through the tissue paper for a clue. Finding none she faced her mother. "Mother, who in the world?"

Sara was white as a sheet. "I am afraid it was—Uncle Wade."

Kathleen sparkled, "How adorable! But how did he know?"

"I told him—that you didn't like me in the black lace."

She expected a thunderbolt. She had broken the family code. She had complained of them to an outsider!

But no thunderbolt came. "Of course we like you in anything!" Kathleen emphasized. "It's only that we want to be proud of you." She was radiant with satisfaction.

But Sara was not radiant. "Of course I can't keep it," she said.

"Mother!"

"My dear, if Wade sent it, it was a lovely thing for him to do. But I can't accept it. You must see that. I can't wear it, and I won't."

"Oh, gee," Randy's voice was sharp, "I should think you'd want to please us."

And Kathleen sank down on the floor beside the box and sobbed, "If you don't wear it, I'll die."

Sara wore the blue dress to the party. She wore the fan and slippers. She received the guests and was a gracious and charming hostess.

When Wade came she said to him, "You shouldn't have done it. But we'll talk about that later."

She was very busy after that and only danced with him once. "I must be nice to other people," she said, "and I've got to find partners for all the wallflowers."

It was when supper was almost over that she disappeared. Wade, hunting for her, finally asked Kathleen, "Where's your mother?"

Kathleen, having the time of her life, said casually, "Oh, she's around somewhere."

But she was not around somewhere.

He went to look for Martha. But nobody had seen Martha. The caterers were packing preparatory to loading up their truck. Presently the party would be over.

And meanwhile, no Sara. No Martha.

Wade made his way to the room where the younger children slept, at the end of the apartment. They had had their refreshments early, had been tucked into bed.

The door of the children's room was shut. Wade opened it and peered in. By the low light he could see that it was empty!

Back he went through all the rooms. There was no place where the four of them could hide, Sara and Martha and Bobby and Mary Virginia. Making his worried way back to the living room, Wade found the guests leaving.

One of the caterer's men, approaching Wade, handed him a letter. "I was to give it to you, sir," he said, "when the evening was over."

Wade opened it and read it. He waited until the last guest had departed, then he said to Kathleen and Randy, "Your mother has gone. She left a letter."

They looked at him with startled faces. *"Gone?"*

"Yes." He read the letter to them while they sat huddled side by side on the sofa like two frightened children.

And this is what Sara had to say: "I didn't want to spoil the party, so I wore the dress. But I am enclosing a Liberty Bond for fifty dollars. It won't cover the entire cost, but I will have more for you later. And you must take it, Wade. I simply can't let you buy a dress for me, although it was dear of you to want to do it, and to try to help me.

"Tell Kathleen and Randy not to worry. The babies and I have gone to find Christmas and we are taking Martha. Aunt Ruth sent me a check for a present and insisted that I spend it on myself, so I am spending it this way, and I'll be back when I am really rested and when I can work things out a little. I know I should have worked them out long ago, but I haven't and I make no apologies. I leaned for so many years on Daddy, and it hasn't been easy not to lean. I am afraid I haven't been a wise mother.

"That's all, and Kathleen and Randy can eat up the rest of the party, and there's money enough in my black bag in the top dresser drawer for immediate expenses."

Wade, looking up with accusing eyes, said, "You see?"

Yet in spite of his sternness he was sorry for the stricken pair. "The trouble was," he told them, "that you were thinking of your mother as a parent and not as a person. You couldn't realize that before she was a mother she was a little clinging child. Your father knew it and cherished her, and when he was taken away she had no one to cling to, and her tendrils of affection have been groping about trying to find support."

In their young eyes was dawning comprehension of a mother who needed to be shielded by their tenderness, upheld by their strength.

"We didn't know," they said.

"You might have known if you hadn't been such a darned pair of egotists," Wade rapped out, "but I suppose you've had to go through with it like measles and whooping cough."

Kathleen, having no fight left in her, wailed, "We can't have Christmas without her."

"No," Wade agreed, "we can't." Then, "Of course, she's gone to Solomon's Shore."

"She wanted us to go," Randy confessed disconsolately, "but Kits wouldn't give up her party."

"Randy!" Kathleen cried, "you wanted it as much as I did."

"Oh, I know. But I didn't dream—" His voice trailed off. Then with an effort: "When she comes back we're going to make it up to her."

"No," Wade told him, "you can't ever make it up to her. Not in the way you think. I'm going to marry her. She doesn't know it. But I do. I've been in love with her for a thousand years. And the pair of you need a father."

At Solomon's Shore, before the dawn on Christmas morning, the stars shone in a sky of misty blue that was merged into a misty sea.

Sara, with Bobby and Mary Virginia, walked under that wide sky and talked in hushed tones.

"Mother, I can hear the world listening," said the imaginative Mary Virginia.

"For what, my darling?"

"For the glad tidings." Mary Virginia was walking, as it were, emotionally on tiptoe.

Sara wondered. Was the world listening? Did it care? Had the Babe of Bethlehem any more than a mystical meaning to the millions who this morning would celebrate His birth?

Bobby was saying, "I want to sing."

As they turned back at last toward home, Bobby trudged along beside his mother, but Mary Virginia ran on ahead, and suddenly she stopped, and piped up alone the song which the choir had sung on the day when Sara had flung at it her bitter challenge.

> *"O little flock,*
> *What words can tell,*
> *The bliss of souls,*
> *Christ loves so well."*

When the song was finished, the tears were running down Sara's cheeks. Oh, her little flock! How could she have dreamed of spending Christmas without all of them! Well, she wouldn't! She wouldn't!

There was a telegraph office at the little station at Solomon's Shore. The station was a squat edifice, and as Sara hurried toward it over the dunes, the light in its window shone low like another star.

"Where are we going, Mother?" Mary Virginia demanded.

"To send a telegram to Uncle Wade."

"What are you going to send it for?"

"It's a secret."

"Oh, a nice secret?"

"A lovely one."

They were satisfied with that. Christmas was a time for lovely secrets.

When they reached the house, Sara went into the kitchen, where old Martha was dishing up the children's cereal. "Martha," she said, "we're going to have six for dinner."

Old Martha asked, "Who's going to eat with you?"

Sara flushed. "I telegraphed Wade to bring the children down."

"If they was mine," said old Martha disapprovingly, "they'd eat lean this day."

"Martha," Sara told her, "you know you're glad they're coming."

"I may be glad," Martha agreed, "but I know what's good for 'em."

Well, after breakfast Sara went out with the children, and they cut down a very small tree, and brought it in and set it up and popped corn at the fireplace, and strung it in snowy chains and hung some old ornaments on it which they found in the attic, and some tiny wax candles salvaged from the same place, and some red apples which Martha had brought with her.

And it was when the turkey was all brown and beautiful in the pan, and the giblets bubbled in the rich gravy, and the mashed potatoes were in a white fluff, and the scalloped oysters plump and delectable under their buttered crumbs, that Wade Phillips' motor car drove up to the doorway.

And Randy and Kathleen, rushing in, hugged their mother; and Wade, following them, put his hands on Sara's shoulders and said, "Did you think we'd let you spend Christmas without us?"

"That's why I telegraphed!"

They chorused, *"Telegraphed?"*

"Yes. Didn't you get it?"

"No. We started early." Then suddenly Kathleen began to cry, great tearing sobs. "Oh, Mumsie," she said, "then you *really* wanted us?"

"Wanted you?" said Sara, and they clung together.

At dinner Wade sat at the head of the table and carved the turkey. Sara sat at the foot, and she told them how they had bought everything after midnight at a market shop where the man was just turning out his lights, but turned them on again to find a turkey for them and oysters and all the other things.

And how they'd taken a late express train to the junction, and a rackety car from there; and how it was too late for Santa Claus, and they had had to trim their own tree!

Then Wade said, "It isn't too late for Santa Claus. At the very last moment he dropped a lot of boxes in my automobile."

And after they had had their mince pie, he brought them in, big boxes and little boxes, and fat boxes and thin boxes, and long boxes and short boxes, and in the boxes was everything that Bobby and Mary Virginia had ever wished for in their young lives, and a lot of things for Kits and Randy.

But there was only one box for Sara, and that was a lavender one with a bunch of violets in it, and there was a book which wasn't very new and had a bookmark in it.

And when in the afternoon Randy and Kathleen went for a walk, and the children were tucked into bed for much-needed naps, Wade and Sara sat by the fire, and outside, over the sea, the sun was going down in a burning glory, and inside there was dimness and the glow of the burning logs.

Then Wade said, "Read what I've marked in the book."

And Sara opened it and read with a shake in her voice:

"And it's buy a bunch of violets for your lady.
While the sky burns blue above. . . .
On the other side the street you'll find it shady. . . .
But buy a bunch of violets for your lady. . . .
And tell her she's your own true love!"

And when she finished, Wade laid his hand over her little one and said, "I've loved you for a thousand years."

And Sara, curling her fingers up to meet his own, felt her burdens fall from her, for in the grasp of that big hand was a promise of a strength to lean on, of a wisdom to look up to and of a tenderness which would follow her ranging lambs and bring them back again to the safe shelter of the fold.

•

One of America's leading novelists and short-story writers during the first half of the twentieth century, **Temple Bailey** (1868–1953) has never gone out of vogue.

GOOD WILL TOWARD MEN

HARRY HARRISON KROLL

Dave liked his teaching job, but the Westbrooks, especially Simon, made his life a hell. And now the crowning blow: a legal warrant for cutting a Christmas tree on the Westbrook property! Good will toward men, indeed!

*T*he Westbrooks were a disagreeable, grasping lot, *Dave Conley was thinking, as he crunched through the snow toward the tree. He was a tall, well-knit young man, with a strong face, fine gray-blue eyes, and a chin turned with resolution, mixed with tenderness. He was garbed in old hunting clothes, with high-laced boots. Reaching the holly tree, he examined it from every angle.

"It's just the thing" he said, half aloud. "But I'd better be sure if it's off the Westbrook land." He was familiar with the land lines and fences; after some search he saw ax marks in a big poplar near by—three chips and a cross.

That's the line, he thought. In a moment he fell to work, and soon had the tree down. He trimmed it with considerable care, chopped off the base evenly and made ready to drag it down to the wagon waiting at the foot of the hill. He took only a few minutes to drag the tree down. He left it on a rock ledge and drove the wagon to a point where he could gently roll the tree on. He was ready to take it to the schoolhouse, where tomorrow the pupils would put it up and decorate it, making ready for the big event of the Yule tree.

Dave Conley returned to his earlier thinking. He would use huge, laughing, grasping Simon Westbrook for Santa as usual. Simon Westbrook had been Santa now for six or seven years—or was it eight? At any rate, Simon was fat, he had a hearty laugh, and if ever anybody got pleasure out of playing a part, it was Simon playing big generous Santa Claus. Once Dave had a suspicion that it was because Simon could give away many presents without the necessity of having to put out any money for them; but as that was rather unkind he didn't harbor the conviction for long.

Dave Conley had gone away to college, come back home, and the school board had given him, the past autumn, a place to teach. The Westbrook clan fought him tooth and nail. They knew a thousand ways to annoy the teacher, and at times young Dave thought that the Westbrook tribe used the whole thousand, plus a few extra combinations for bad measure. They talked about him; they said the scholars got into fights on the grounds and to and fro from school; they disapproved of the long recesses. Sometimes Dave did forget and go overtime a few moments when the play was full of fun. They magnified every little failing, and overlooked entirely the fact that Dave Conley had the school in splendid enthusiasm, with plenty of hard work during study hours. Best of all, his scholars loved him. Even one or two of the Westbrook girls and boys secretly loved Dave. They dared not admit that at home, of course.

Dave hauled the tree on down to the schoolhouse where he unloaded it. He then drove the team on to his boarding place, at Ham Ricks, where he put it up. He had been home perhaps an hour when Squire Leverage, chairman of the school board, drove up to the gate in the wintry sunlight and called.

"Hay, 'fessor!"

Dave went out to the gate. "Come in, Uncle Jesse."

"Nope, got to be riding. I dropped by to tell you I won't be able to help with the tree—called away on sickness; so I'm just going to turn all my official jobs over to you. You see about getting the Santa, and Mis' Laws has the red suit up at her house. I been thinking about Sim Westbrook. He's awful good at the job, but them Westbrooks haven't done a thing all fall but make trouble, so I'd made up my mind not to let them come in and run the show. So you get up Santa—I'll just leave it to you. If I get back in time I hope to come to the tree. So long, and good luck. Hope you have a grand time."

"Thanks, Squire—we shall."

Squire Leverage drove away. He had been gone less than five minutes when Morris Jones, the constable, came up on horseback. Dave turned at the call, thinking, whimsically, that it was a busy day for him.

"Hello, Mr Jones. 'Light and come in."

"Thankee, Dave—I got a little business here with you. Some papers." He was hesitant, as he fumbled in his pockets.

"Papers?" said Dave, in surprise.

"Warrant. Swore out in Squire Jake Westbrook's co't. I didn't much want to serve it, but duty is duty—you know how them things is, 'fessor."

The young man stood there a bit stupefied. "Warrant!" he repeated, in a tight voice. "For *what?*"

The constable produced the legal paper, and read the charge. "For willfully stealing a tree off Simon and Clay Westbrook's land."

"Why—why—" gasped Dave. "Tree! You mean, that Christmas tree? Why, my goodness, they must have broken some necks to get this warrant sworn out, for it's only been two hours since I cut the tree. Besides, it's not from their land. I looked carefully for the lines."

"I'm skeered," said Jones, doubtfully, "that you made some kind of a mistake, 'fessor, for the tree shore did come off the Westbrook land. I rode by the place to make sure where it happened, and everything. He was standing behind another tree, no piece at all off, and he seen you cutting it, him and another feller. I know you didn't mean no harm, 'fessor, but that's the way it is, and I'm sort of skeered that it may mess you up right smart, if they keep pushing it. You know what sort of folks they are—stubborn, hard-headed, and once they've put their mean hands to the plow, they bust out the middle or bust up the plow."

"I know," said Dave Conley, for the first time with a hint of bitterness. "Well, I reckon there's nothing I can do about it but face it out. I dread it, though—on account of the school. I should have had sense enough to make sure."

"If it had happened on this side the line, you could get the case in Jedge Leverage's co't. He'd throw it out, and throw out Simon Westbrook, too. But since it's going to go through the Westbrook hands in trial, it's going to be a right smart mess. Most folks, 'fessor, will take your side. Don't worry."

"All the same, the trial is bound to react against the school."

"Y-yes, that's right. To some extent. But fight it out. Don't let 'em put anything over on you. Here's the bond. Sign it. Get somebody to go on with you, or you can give me a signed check for the amount of bond to appear two weeks from now before Squire Jake Westbrook."

Dave signed the papers, wrote the check, and the constable turned and went back as he had come.

The whole disagreeable affair took the flavor out of the Christmas season for young Dave Conley. "Peace on earth, good will toward men"—what irony it was! The fact that the incident was merely technical guilt did not matter. He should have taken more care. To that extent he certainly was blameworthy. Nor was it of any moment that the tree itself was worth little or nothing. He had taken something off somebody's property, without permission. Perhaps the tree, cut and trimmed and taken to the city, would have fetched two dollars. The ugliness of a small matter magnified into a big one was that which annoyed Dave.

While the scholars put up the tree in the schoolhouse, and the big girls decorated it beautifully with colored papers and glass ornaments, Dave Conley watched with a sense of moroseness. All the Yuletide sweetness was gone from him.

Meanwhile, of course, in the Westbrook camp was a good amount of gratification. Simon Westbrook, throwing out his barrel chest, would smite himself heroically, and laugh in that vast manner he had: "I ketched the 'fessor on his blind side that time, and socked him one that'll hold him a spell!" Then his face hardened. His eyes glinted. "He thinks he's some pumpkins—go off and take on a jag of book-l'arning, then come back and gooly over us pore folks! He ain't such-a-much, nohow."

Minnie Westbrook, one of the younger girls who secretly had succumbed to the charms of the schoolmaster, came home that afternoon and reported to big, gloating Simon:

"You're not going to be any Santa Claus this time, Sim!" she said, with a certain ferocity.

"Who said I won't!" bellowed Simon.

"I said you won't!"

"Yah, I guess you're boss man of the works, eh? Well, I'll pull your pigtails out and throw you in the creek, if you get sassy with Sim Westbrook. I'll reach down and gnaw off two-three acres of that bigoted upper lip of your'n. How come I won't be Santa? I already asked Squire Jesse Leverage, and he never said no word against it."

"Well, Judge Jesse he's gone away till after Christmas, and gave 'Fessor Dave the right to name his own Santa!"

"What?" barked Simon.

"I told you!" said the girl fiercely. "You just made a mess of things, and yourself, too, when you started that lawsuit!"

His dark face went a curious gray, then became swept with the swarth of chagrined anger. "Say—" began Simon; then he fell to raving and growling. "So that's the way he worked to get it back on me! He knowed I wanted to be that Santy. He knowed good and well it's my job. I been so now for eight years. Everybody in the settlement knows it's my job. The suit fits me like it was made for me. I do it far better than any other person in these parts. Dave Conley knows that. He knows how I feel. Now—great guns!" He stopped, glaring at his sister, as if she might have some part in it. "I'm half a mind to box your jaws! I'm going to see the other members of the school board."

"Well, I hope they don't give it to you!"

"You say that again, and I'll snatch you bald-headed."

"I hope," said the girl, "they don't give it to you! You're just plain mean and small, that's what, Sim Westbrook! If you had an inch of real man in you, you'd go straight to Grandpap Westbrook and have that case thrown out of court, and you'd go to that Christmas tree and apologize in public for what you've done!"

"I'm a mind to wring your neck!" He did nothing of the kind; instead, he hurried out, saddled his mule, and rode furiously away to interview the other members of the school board.

He came back, after an hour, looking glum and browbeaten. He had talked with Mr. Walker, and Luke Sardis, the other members; they said it was Judge Jesse Leverage's job to look after that. If Judge Jesse had empowered Mr. Dave to get his Santa, then Mr. Dave should get him, and that was all there was of it.

To anyone not familiar with the singletrack mountaineer mind it would be difficult to understand how desperately upset Simon Westbrook was by the turn of events. Few honors were to be had in the simplicity of life in Poverty Run and Chittling Meat Mountain. The adults divided the honors of magistrate's office, constable and school board among them. Little was left for an arrogant, power-hungry young fellow like Simon Westbrook. Moreover, he was the best Santa that could be had in that locality. The honest truth was, he was a genuine artist at it.

Now he had played havoc. He had lost the single great honor that he wanted, above all others available to him. He could not humble himself to Dave Conley, however. That would have been unthinkable. He beat his hands together, and moaned, walking up and down the big puncheon-floored room of the mountain dwelling.

"I wisht I'd never have started this mess! I wisht that idiot of Dave Conley had a-left that tree alone, then I wouldn't done this! I'm of a mind to go hunt him up and beat his head for him. It was all his fault!"

"It's your fault!" accused his sister.

"Look here! You going back on your own blood and kin on account of that there feller?"

"I aim to be fair. All the pupils are crazy about 'Fessor Dave. He's nice, and he's smart, and he's good. He wouldn't ever have sworn out a warrant for you, Sim! If he'd been back of that tree, watching you cut a tree on his land, he'd have yelled out to you, 'Don't do that, Sim!' or, more apt, he'd have come on down and said, 'Take it. It's a nice tree. I'm glad I can give it to you and to the school. Here, let me help you cut it and load it.' That's what he'd have said, I think!"

Simon glowered at Minnie, in baffled rage. "You done fell in love with the teacher! Think of that!"

"No!" she denied swiftly. "But I've got a right to like somebody that I ought to like."

"I'm going to hunt that feller up and have this thing out with him!" The matter had resolved itself in Simon's mind as a personal issue. He went to the door and took the gun from the horns above. Minnie undertook to wrestle the weapon from him, but he flung her backward, and strode out into the falling dusk. A light snow was falling; the wind was bitter in its knife thrusts. Simon Westbrook, but dimly aware he was making an idiot of himself, walked quickly down the school path. He thought that he probably would find young Dave there, working on the tree. Christmas Eve would be tomorrow night. Tomorrow night! He stumbled. The wind held him back; then he took a fresh grip on his anger, and pushed on.

Men had killed each other for less. The Mosley-Westbrook feud, famous in its day, had cost a score of lives over the years on a pretext no more valid than Simon Westbrook's. The excuse does not count much in anger; the condition of mind and drive of anger is all that counts. This set and drive carried Simon Westbrook on.

He saw a dim, muscular form take shape in the twilight of ghostly snow. Simon Westbrook stopped. The figure came up the trail, carrying some sort of parcel. Simon stiffened all through his great frame, and he brought the gun to rest in the bend of his arm.

"Howdy," he snarled, standing in the middle of the path.

"Well, how're you?"

Although Dave Conley was startled by this unexpected encounter with Simon Westbrook his voice was still quiet and pleasant. He saw that Simon was armed. In that grim, swift moment, the schoolmaster sensed that Simon was after him.

Young Westbrook stood erect. "I—I—" he said, through set teeth; "I could kill you!" The barrel of the gun came gently to a point where it covered Dave Conley.

"Why, certainly," agreed Dave, and he was glad that his voice was natural and pleasant, though he knew a quarrel was inevitable, and that it would almost as inevitably cause this simple fellow to kill him. "I suppose," he went on quietly, "you could take that gun, and kill the next dozen men, women and children you met. What of it? It wouldn't show you up as much of a man."

"That's what you say!" snarled Simon.

"Anyway, what are you sore about? You had a right to prosecute me for getting that tree. I had no legal right to go on your land and take what was yours. I'm not kicking. I could have wished that the whole unfortunate matter was otherwise, but I cannot deny those rights that are so patently yours. And about acting Santa Claus, I've brought the suit to you."

Simon looked dazed, and he eyed the bundle with befuddled eyes. "That?"

"That's it. You're the best man for the job. You're an artist at it in fact, Simon. You're not much on the peace-on-earth-good-will-toward-men side of it, going around here toting guns to shoot unarmed school-teachers. But I have to admit the truth and say that you're the finest Santa I ever saw or heard of. So, I kept thinking, and I finally made up my mind that I could do nothing except give the job to the one best suited for it, whether I liked you or not, personally, Simon. The truth is, I don't. I can't, but I believe that I can be honest with myself and you, and at the same time give you the job I know you want.

"Here's the suit." Dave put it in Simon's limp arms. "I suppose some folks will say that I'm acting the coward, trying to buy off your anger. It may be, Simon, you will think so. I can't help what others say. I hope that I am anything but a coward. I'm asking you to take your old place for no reason in the world save that you're by far the best for it. The job is small; I think the principle of the thing is very great." He turned after a moment, leaving the dazed Simon standing in the snowy gloom, and retraced his steps.

The next evening the crowd came early to the schoolhouse, and soon the room was packed. The tree was genuinely beautiful in its decorations and burden of presents. Santa was late. When he entered, he was badly out of breath. In his vigorous, robust voice, curiously changed from the tense savage tone Dave had last heard, Santa said, "I been late, I had to stop down beyond the fence row and pray a spell. Pray for this here Christmas season, pray for all you leetle chaps and the big folks too; but mostly I had to get on my hunkers and pray for myself. And I had a right smart rassle with the bad in myself, at that. I don't mind telling all you folks—big ones and little ones, too. Some will know better than others what I mean. But this here thing we call Christmas is time for peace and good will. And I ain't been so peaceful, in my heart, and they ain't been such a power of good will in me—till I had it out just now in the fence corner. So, before Santa starts giving out the presents, I got a few different kinds of presents to give.

"Take this here lovely tree, chilluns. It belonged, so I hear tell, to a low-down, mean-headed feller named Simon Westbrook. He got a lawsuit going over it, against the school-teacher. Well, Santa went to the jedge and say to the jedge, 'Throw that case out of co't.' So the jedge he say, 'Okeh, I'll throw it out of co't.' And he did. Now, me, Santa, gives the tree to the school and the 'fessor. And the 'fessor, I might as well tell you all, is a right smart feller. He teeched a grand school here, and will keep on at such. Now, let's give all of you a pretty gift!"

What it cost Simon Westbrook to say this not many would ever know. Dave Conley knew; he was sensitive to human ways, and he appreciated with keen depth the greatness that Simon showed. Perhaps no one else than Dave could have caused this change, for that was a part of the young schoolmaster's genius. At any rate the yuletide spirit prevailed—peace on earth, and good will toward men.

The wintry wind, whipping the eaves of the old schoolhouse, seemed to repeat it: *"Peace on earth . . . good will toward men . . ."*

•

Harry Harrison Kroll (1888–1967) was a prolific novelist and short-story writer during much of the twentieth century. He specialized in stories set in Appalachia.

THE HOUSE THAT GLOWED

ARTHUR MAXWELL

It was bitterly cold that Christmas Eve, and the freezing little boy had been turned away at house after house. Finally, he concluded that there was no alternative but to die in the snow.

Yet there was one house left—a tiny tumble-down cottage. Hoping against hope, he decided to try one last time.

It was Christmas Eve, and poor little Johann, driven out of his home by an angry and brutal step-father, was trudging wearily through the snow.

His ragged coat was shodden with melted snow. His shoes were split at the seams, so that his feet were damp and numb with cold. His quaint cap, pulled well down over his ears and forehead, had a gaping tear that let in the biting wind.

Night was falling, and the gathering darkness found the homeless little boy still plodding on his sad and lonely way.

If only I could find some shelter, some place where I could get warm, and the wind would not chill me so, he thought to himself. *If only someone would give me some food to eat and something hot to drink!*

Coming to the edge of the forest, he caught sight of a little village nestling in the valley below, with several fine, large houses dotting the hills around it. Lights were already twinkling in the windows, while the smoke from many chimneys, curling upward, blended with the murky sky.

A great new hope sprang up in little Johann's heart. Here at last, among so many lovely homes, he would surely find someone to care for him. He walked more quickly, certain that his troubles were almost over.

Soon he came to the entrance of a fine, big mansion. There were many lights in the windows and a very bright one over the front door. *Surely,* he thought, *people who could live in such a house must have lots of money and would be only too pleased to help a poor, hungry little boy."*

Very bravely he walked up to the front door, and by standing on tiptoe, managed to reach the bell. He pushed it hard, and there was such a noise inside that it frightened him. But he was more frightened still when the great oak door was thrown back and a big man dressed in a fine blue and gold uniform looked out at him.

"Did you ring that bell?" asked the haughty butler, frowning.

"Y-y-y-yes," stammered Johann. "I-I-I'm very cold and hungry, and I thought you—"

"This is Christmas Eve," snapped the butler, "and the house is full of guests. I'm sorry, but we haven't time to bother with the likes of you just now. Good night."

And the door was shut.

Oh! said Johann to himself, *I never thought anyone would do that. But perhaps they are too busy here. I must try somewhere else.*

So he walked on down into the village itself, passing by the other big mansions for fear the people inside might also be too busy to care about a hungry little boy on Christmas Eve.

From the first house he reached there came sounds of music and laughter. *These people will be friendly,* he said to himself as he knocked gently on the door. But there was so much noise inside that he had to knock again and again, each time louder than before.

At last the door swung open, and a young man wearing a funny paper cap looked out.

"Excuse me," said Johann, "but I wondered if you could—"

"Sorry," cried the jovial young man, "we're having a great Christmas Eve party in here, and we can't stop now."

"But please, please!" pleaded Johann.

"Sorry. Good night!" cried the young man. And bang! The door was shut.

Terribly disappointed, Johann went next door, but the people there were making so much noise that they didn't even hear him at all, loud as he knocked.

At the next house a crabby old gentleman looked out an upstairs window and told him to run home and not bother the neighbors. Run home, indeed!

At another house he was told to call again another day. They would help him then perhaps, the people said. But he needed help *now!*

So, going from house to house through the entire village, he sought shelter and food, and found none.

Almost hopeless and heartbroken, he trudged on into the night, leaving the twinkling lights behind hm. He felt he could lie down and die in the road, he was so tired, so hungry, so discouraged.

Just then he happened to look up and found himself passing a tiny, tumble-down old cottage, so dark and dismal that he probably wouldn't have seen it at all but for the white carpet of snow on the ground showing it up. A blind almost covered the one window letting a faint streak of light show through at the bottom.

Johann stood still and wondered what he should do.

Should he knock here?

What would be the use? Surely if the people who lived in all the big houses—who had money for lovely parties and things—couldn't afford to help a poor boy, how could the folks in a house like this? No, it was of no use. Better not bother them. Better go on and die in the woods.

Then he thought again. He had knocked at so many houses, there could be no harm in trying one more. So he turned from the road up the snow-covered garden path and tapped gently on the door.

A moment later the door opened cautiously, and an elderly woman peered out. "Bless my soul!" she exclaimed. "Whatever are you doing out there in the cold tonight?"

"Please—" began Johann.

But before he could say another word she had flung the door wide open and dragged him inside.

"You poor little child!" she exclaimed. "Deary, deary me! You look so cold and hungry. Half starved, or I'm mistaken. And wet clear through. Let's get those things off at once. Wait a moment while I stir up the fire and put the kettle on."

Johann looked about him and saw that the little one-room cottage was as bare as could be, without even a carpet on the floor. The light he had seen came from one lone candle set on the mantelpiece. But he hadn't time to see much else, for the kind woman was soon stripping off his wet rags, wrapping him in a blanket, and setting him up at the table before a bowl of steaming soup.

Then she went back to stir the pot on the stove. As she did so she suddenly noticed that something strange was happening. She looked up.

Was it a dream, or were her eyes deceiving her? The candlelight had given place to a warm and lovely glow that seemed to be getting brighter every minute, filling every corner of the cottage with a heavenly radiance. Every drab piece of furniture seemed to be shining and glistening like burnished gold, as when God filled the temple with His glory.

And the rich man, looking down from his mansion on the hill, suddenly exclaimed. "There's a strange light in the valley. Look! Widow Greatheart's cottage is on fire!"

The news spread swiftly from house to house, and soon all the merry parties were abandoned as the people, wrapping themselves up in their coats and shawls, rushed out to see what was the matter.

They saw the light, too, and running toward the widow's cottage, beheld the poor tumble-down old building glowing like an alabaster bowl. Very excited, they gathered around it.

Peering inside, all they could see was the dear old woman caring for the very same little boy who had called that night at so many of their homes.

Then, as the light faded, they knocked on the door to ask anxiously what could have happened.

"I really don't know," said Widow Greatheart, with a smile of wondrous joy and satisfaction on her face. "I just seemed to hear a voice saying to me, 'Inasmuch as you have done it unto one of the least of these My children, you have done it unto Me.'"

•

Arthur Maxwell (1896–1970) spent the first forty years of his life in England and the last thirty-four in America. One of the most prolific writers of his time, he wrote 112 books that have been printed in 56 languages. A staggering total of 85,000,000 of his books have sold.

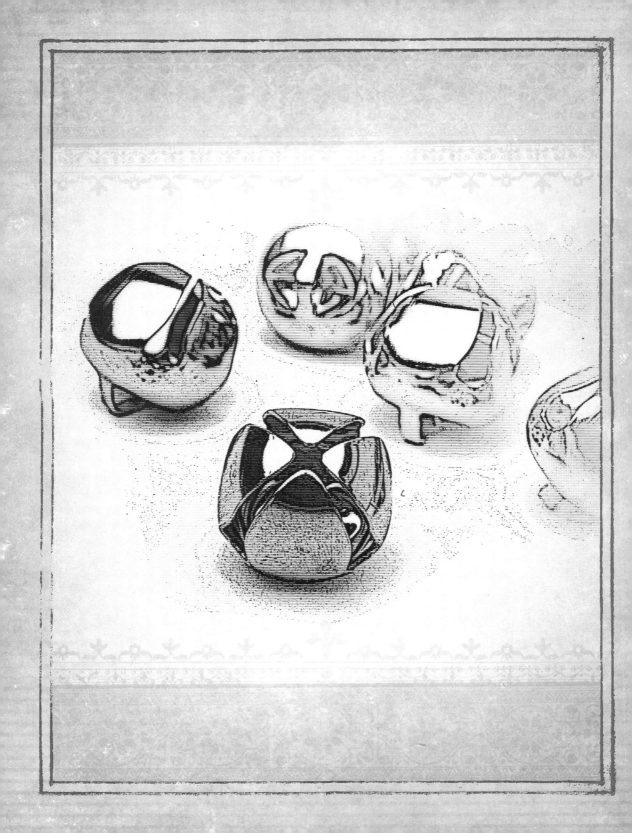

BOBO AND THE CHRISTMAS SPIRIT

EDITH BALLINGER PRICE

In Red Rose Troop there were two forces always at work: Jane Burke's everlasting desire to do everything according to the book; and Bobo Witherspoon, as unpredictable and spontaneous as it's possible for any human to be.

And now Bobo was at it again.

Bobo Witherspoon was forever upsetting the ordered life of Red Rose Troop—which, but for her, would have gone on almost entirely along the lines laid down for it by Jane Burke, who liked to do things according to a pattern. Bobo, being much the youngest member of the troop, was expected—quite naturally—to have no say-so in its doings. But whatever else she did, Bobo certainly did not live according to plan. Whatever pattern she followed was made as fresh as each day's dawn, and people with orderly minds like Jane Burke's simply cannot understand that sort of thing.

Therefore, when Bobo strolled in to the first autumn meeting of Red Rose Troop one particularly sultry September afternoon, singing "The First Noel," it distinctly jarred on Jane's sensibilities.

"What on earth do you mean by that unseasonable yelping?" she demanded sharply.

Bobo looked pained. "It's just that I'm full of the Christmas spirit," she said.

Jane, Lillian, and Vera hooted at her in unison.

"Christmas spirit!" Jane cried. "I haven't recovered from Labor Day yet!"

Bobo looked distant and dreamy. "But it's there," she said. "I can get right into it any minute I want to. In fact, I have a hard time not being full of the Christmas spirit all year round."

"My dear child," Jane enunciated firmly, "we have hikes to consider just now. Hikes—and then the cookie sale, and our harvest party, and Thanksgiving, and—"

"And then Christmas," said Bobo softly.

"I think planning for the troop can safely be left to its senior members," Jane remarked rather acidly. Time was fleeting.

But Bobo's singular obsession was persistent.

"Can't we do something about it?" Ruthie Kent complained to Jane a couple of weeks later. "She warbles 'Deck the Halls with Boughs of Holly' while she pulls the cornstalks. She bawls 'Jolly Old Saint Nicholas' while she cuts jack-o'-lanterns. It makes me feel as if I were going down too fast in an elevator."

Ruthie looked at her queerly.

"Good gracious!" cried Jane. "What was I singing?"

"'It Came Upon a Midnight Clear,'" said Ruthie.

Jane clutched her brow in horror. "How can such *things be?*" she groaned. It was actually with some effort that she rallied herself and the troop to the work in hand. "Don't let your defenses down for a moment," she warned the others. "This thing is insidious."

So when Bobo arrived at the meeting a little before Thanksgiving, with a sprig of artificial holly in her buttonhole and a string of small bells jingling on her cap, Red Rose Troop bent determinedly over the cornshock they were arranging in a corner of the gym, and attempted to ignore her. But the bells pervaded the atmosphere with a frosty tinkle that was infectious.

"Jingle bells, jingle bells, jingle all the way!" hummed Red, tucking the pumpkin at the foot of the cornshock.

"Oh, what fun it is to ride in a one-horse open sleigh!" The troop took it up, and the room rocked.

"Stop it! Stop that immediately!" cried Jane. She cleared her throat and began to shout a counteractive strain.

The resultant discord was hideous. Jane stopped her ears and sang on with characteristic determination.

Bobo was not singing either ditty. She was sitting quietly in a corner, stitching away clumsily on a length of red muslin. It was not long before Jane spied her.

"And what is that, may I ask?" she demanded, taking her fingers out of her ears.

"Christmas stocking for an orphan," said Bobo promptly. "I have loads of the stuff. We can all make them."

"We are going to make scrapbooks," Jane announced, "for the children at the hospital."

"I thought it would be nice to make stockings," said Bobo, "and fill them with candies and jokes and things."

Several girls sat down near Bobo and inspected the pieces of red material that bulged from her workbag.

"What do you plan to put in these things?" Vera asked.

"Well," Bobo said, laying down her stocking for she could not possibly talk and sew at once, "I thought we could make some candy. And then, if we spent fifteen or twenty cents, we could get some little toys. And then we could make tiny little joke books with things cut out and pasted in, for each stocking—and put in some peanuts and popcorn, and things like a stringknitter or a puzzle."

"They'll have to be bushel baskets instead of stockings, won't they?" Lillian said.

Helen had picked up a length of red stuff and Bobo's scissors, and was chopping out a foot-shaped piece. She was absently humming "We Three Kings of Orient Are."

Red joined her, rummaging for thread, and soon half the troop was measuring and snipping and basting. Jane, her jaw set defiantly, advanced in solitary state upon the cornshock languishing in its corner, and put some ostentatious finishing touches to it.

But Bobo's great inspiration did not come to her until one day when she happened to be chatting with her friend, Mr. Horatio Bristle. No one else dared to chatter to Mr. Bristle; he had always cherished a reputation for being a rather formidable curmudgeon. Bobo's ability to wind him around her little finger never ceased to astonish her comrades. Always awed by him, they never got beyond, "Yes, Mr. Bristle," and "No, Mr. Bristle," if called upon to converse with him.

On this mild day of belated Indian summer the old gentleman was out in his garden, seeing if the half-hardy perennials were properly mulched, and admiring a few bronze chrysanthemums which had weathered the earlier frost.

"Ho, Bobo!" he called to his young friend over the fence. "D'ye like raw turnips? If you pull hard enough, I expect you can get one out of what's left of the vegetable patch."

Anything in the line of food appealed to Bobo. A raw turnip that has been touched by frost is a pungently appetizing affair. Bobo tugged one up, rubbed it off, and bit into it appreciatively.

Mr. Bristle eyed askance the one she pulled up and offered him.

"Hm, well," he mused, "I used to like 'em when I was a boy. After a day's gunning, I'd come across 'em in a field. Never will forget how good they tasted." He looked about him surreptitiously and took an experimental bite.

It was while they were thus engaged munching earthy turnips that Bobo's great thought came to her. "Mr. Bristle!" she cried. "I don't know why I've never noticed it before. Have you ever thought how much you look like Santa Claus?"

"Hey?" cried the astonished gentleman, choking over his turnip. "Santa Claus, did you say?"

"Yes!" exclaimed Bobo, her eyes growing rounder and rounder as she gazed. "Your face is so nice and red—and your mustache is so white. All you'd need would be a beard and the proper clothes. You're just the right shape—I mean, you wouldn't need any pillows or anything."

"Hrrumph!" snorted Mr. Bristle. "I wouldn't, hey?" He patted the front of his waistcoat rather ruefully. "Always meaning to do something about that."

"Oh, don't!" Bobo begged him. "You're just right. Oh, would you, dear Mr. Bristle—would you?"

"Would I what?" he asked suspiciously, backing away.

"Would you be Santa Claus when we go to the hospital to take the children their Christmas stockings?"

"Me? Santa Claus for a bunch of kids?" roared Mr. Bristle. "Jumping snakes, no! D'ye want Horatio Bristle to make an idiot of himself in public? If there's anything I can't abide—"

"It would just be poor little sick children who wouldn't have a proper Christmas," Bobo finished. "You'd only have to hand out the stockings. You wouldn't have to say anything."

"No!" said Mr. Bristle.

"Nobody'd even know who you were," Bobo assured him soothingly.

"No, no, NO!" shouted Mr. Bristle.

Bobo rummaged mournfully among the turnip tops. She began singing "God Rest You Merry, Gentlemen," and then stopped.

"Go ahead, go ahead," said Mr. Bristle. "Sounds pretty. Takes me back."

"I can't go ahead," Bobo told him. "I was full of the Christmas spirit, but now that you won't be Santa Claus, I've sort of lost it all of a sudden."

"Christmas spirit—hmp!" snapped Mr. Bristle. "Feels more like Fourth o' July!" He picked a chrysanthemum and put it in his buttonhole.

"I can smell snow coming, though," sighed Bobo, "or I thought I could. And I could just see you in jolly red clothes, with a little bell on your cap. You do have such nice twinkly blue eyes."

"I suppose you'd like me to grow a beard by December twenty-fifth?" Mr. Bristle suggested, with what he intended for sarcasm.

"That would be wonderful!" cried Bobo. "Though I expect we could paste one on. Oh, then you will do it, Mr. Bristle? You *will!*"

"Never said any such thing!" stormed the outraged old gentleman.

"But you even said you'd grow a long white beard!" Bobo cried joyfully. "Oh, I do like you very much, Mr. Bristle, when you get co-operative!"

Mr Bristle gnawed his mustache. "Well, Christmas is a long way off yet," he muttered evasively. "You never can tell."

"That's a real promise," Bobo interpreted, dancing gleefully in the turnip patch. "Well, good-by! I have to be very busy now, with lots of new plans. Don't really bother about the beard—we can make one."

She climbed over the fence and vanished.

Bobo won, though Jane Burke did her best to steady the situation and make everything conform to the original plan. But by the middle of December, Red Rose Troop was completely out of control. The first snowball turned the trick. Bobo singing carols in September was sufficiently disturbing; Bobo frolicking in, her rosy cheeks flecked with snowflakes, was too much to withstand. The whole troop shouted "Come All Ye Faithful" till the gym echoed. Jane sang along, too.

Bobo checked up on Mr. Bristle and found, to her delighted satisfaction, that he had obtained a handsome red suit and provided himself with a very becoming white beard which could be attached by means of hooks over his ears. He demonstrated it to her, and though the effect when seen with his gray business clothes and wing collar was quite surprising, Bobo approved wholeheartedly.

"Makes me look ten years older," sighed Mr. Bristle, detaching the whiskers and rubbing his pink chin.

"Oh, no!" Bobo assured him. "Younger, I think."

The troop was filled with mingled feelings of astonishment and gratification when Bobo made the spectacular announcement she had been saving up.

"Mr. Bristle is going to be Santa Claus, and hand out the stockings while we sing. Yes, truly—he's promised. And he has his red suit and a lovely woolly beard."

One helpful result of the announcement was that it really finished Jane. She could not insist that the stockings not be sent to the hospital, if the great Mr. Bristle, complete with red suit and whiskers, stood ready to distribute them.

On the morning before Christmas, Mr. Bristle called Bobo by telephone. "Lots o' nice snow piled up for you," he said. "I expect you're pleased. How're you planning to get over to the hospital?"

"Walk, I suppose," Bobo said. "Are your Santa Claus boots rubber ones, Mr. Bristle?"

"They are not!" he roared over the wire. "And Horatio Bristle isn't going to slip and slide through the streets of this town rigged up like that, anyway. How many of you are going?"

"About sixteen," Bobo figured.

"Well," said Mr. Bristle, "if you tell 'em all to meet at my house at five o'clock, I'll have something to convey us."

"Oh, ought you to?" said Bobo, who loved to walk in the snow. "Isn't it pretty skiddy?"

"Did you ever hear of Santa Claus using an automobile?" Mr. Bristle inquired.

"Oh, oh!" cried Bobo, breathless. "You—you don't mean reindeer, do you?"

There was a sort of choking sound from the other end.

At five o'clock, to Bobo's huge delight, snow was again falling softly through the blue winter darkness. No Christmas star—but then, you couldn't have stars and snowfall both at once, except on Christmas cards. Bobo sang as she ran to Mr. Bristle's house, and the bells on her cap jingled. She marveled that they should sound so loud, and so much as real sleighbells must sound. Some echo trick of the snow and the stillness, perhaps. Then, coming down the street, she saw dimly an enormous bobsled, drawn by two stout farm horses. The string of bells around the neck of each jangled rhythmically. She could see a group of Red Rose girls on Mr. Bristle's porch, peering out at the jolly sight, and she ran and joined them to watch the sleigh go by.

But it didn't go by. It pulled up with a hearty, "Whoa!" at Mr. Bristle's gate, and the old gentleman himself, his white woolly beard bobbing above his ample crimson chest, came out of his house and looked about.

"Well, Bobo!" he cried, spying his young friend. "How d'ye like that? Hey? I knew just where I could get it, out in the country. Horatio Bristle didn't propose to wade around in the snowbanks—not to please anybody!"

Bobo was speechless. Miss Roberts said, "I think you must have caught the Christmas spirit, too, Mr. Bristle. We've all been exposed to it now for quite a long time."

"Christmas spirit, hmp!" said Mr. Bristle. But he beamed and chuckled every time he looked at the sleigh. It was a wonderful vehicle and it held all eighteen passengers, sitting on its floor in the sweet-smelling straw.

Mr. Bristle flourished his hand. "Hospital," he commanded.

The driver cracked his whip, and the wonderful, smooth motion began—the quiet gliding that is like no other motion in the world, broken only by the frosty jingle of the bells and the muted thud of the horses' hoofs on the snow. Quiet, that is, until Red Rose Troop began to sing. The Christmas spirit welled up within them till it hurt, and then they sang "Jingle Bells" as it should be sung. People, hurrying with wreaths and last-minute purchases, stopped to look and listen. What a sight it was—the big open sleigh, the two sturdy gray horses, the merry faces, and Santa Claus himself nodding and waving with abandon. Many of the passers-by began to hum, themselves, as they hurried homeward.

"Funny," said Red. "You'd think we'd be there by now. Not that I ever want to stop sleigh riding."

"Horses are slower than automobiles," Jane reminded her instructively.

"Where are we, anyhow?" Vera wondered. It was difficult to see—darkness, and snow stinging the eyes that tried to penetrate it.

Just then there was a blur of light in the swirling flakes, and the sleigh pulled up before the dim bulk of a big hospital building. Everyone tumbled out and surged, stamping and blinking, into the entry.

"Let's park the stockings here," suggested Miss Roberts. "If the children see them first, we'll never be able to sing."

The red stockings were left beside the door, and then Red Rose Troop, still rubbing the snow and darkness from dazzled eyes, found itself suddenly in the bewildering brightness of a large rotunda. Miss Roberts opened her mouth to say they were expected in the children's ward—and it stayed open. The troop became dimly aware of boys in wheel chairs, boys on crutches, boys in maroon dressing gowns walking slowly about the rotunda. They were young men, not children.

"Good gracious!" Miss Roberts gasped. "We're—we're at the Military Hospital! What shall we do?"

"Jumping snakes!" gulped Mr. Bristle. "I just said 'Hospital,' and this is what the driver thought I meant." He began to back towards the entrance door, grappling convulsively with his whiskers. Bobo caught him by his scarlet coat.

"What are you doing?" she whispered urgently. "Where are you going? We have to go on—oh, don't you see? They're all expecting us to!"

"But—" murmured Miss Roberts, looking apprehensively at all the eager grins, as more and more soldiers limped down corridors to the rotunda.

"Come on—come on!" begged Bobo desperately. "Oh, don't let them see we didn't mean it for them!" She began to sing "God Rest You Merry, Gentlemen," and Red Rose Troop joined in, perforce.

Tenors and baritones came in, now—even Mr. Bristle's unexpected and apologetic bass.

There was clapping, and pleased laughter.

"Girl Scouts! Swell of them to come!"

"My kid sister's a Girl Scout. If I was home for Christmas . . ."

"And look at Santa! Gosh, no fake about him!"

There was an appreciative hum as the soldiers gathered around the carolers.

"Sing 'The First Noel'—d'you know that one?"

"We'll come in on the chorus!"

"How about 'O Little Town of Bethlehem'? We always sang that one Christmas Eve, at home."

So there was more singing—lots of it. Carols and marching tunes; and carols again. There was close harmony; there were barbershop chords; the deep voices joining with the troop's soprano melody gave the effect of a whole chorus. And Mr. Bristle found his tongue at last, and cracked jokes and told funny stories. And afterwards, every boy who could do so crowded near the door to see them off.

Outside, the snow had stopped and the stars shone like steel. One of the waiting horses tossed his head, and his string of bells clashed musically.

"I didn't dream it, then," said one boy softly. "Sleighbells! Like I was home in Minnesota."

"Gosh, we surely thank you for coming."

"It was kind of different from anything we've had—we sure appreciate it, ma'am."

"Do you guys remember where we were last Christmas?"

Someone said grimly, "Korea!" and there was a brief silence.

Mr. Bristle cleared his throat violently and cut a sort of caper on the steps. "Merry Christmas to all, and to all a good night!' he cried.

"Hi, Prancer! Hi, Dancer!" shouted one of the boys, as the sleigh pulled away. There was a cheer from the doorway.

Bobo, pulling the carriage robe to her chin, sighed blissfully. "Wasn't it—simply wonderful?" she breathed.

"It turned out all right, I guess," Vera agreed. "There was a bad moment there at the beginning, though."

"It was perfectly simple," Bobo said earnestly, "as soon as everybody got the Christmas spirit."

Miss Roberts and Mr. Bristle exchanged looks.

"Seems to me it was you who made us go on with it, Bobo," Santa Claus remarked.

"No, I just started singing," Bobo said.

"It was certainly fortunate," said Jane, "that we left the stockings outside."

"I think it's too bad we did," Bobo said. "They prob'ly would have loved them."

"And then what would we have had for the children, pray tell?" Jane inquired. "For you may remember that we're still expected at the children's ward."

Bobo refrained from reminding Jane that her original plan had been merely to send scrapbooks. 'She was too busy thinking of the wonderful, unexpected adventure into which the Christmas Spirit had led them; of the pleased, touched faces they had just left behind, and of the small happy faces they would soon see.

"You are so nice, Mr. Bristle," she sighed, "when you get started. All those soldiers thought you really were Santa Claus. I know they did."

"Hm," said the old gentleman, smoothing his woolly whiskers, "by the time I've lived through this evening, I'll begin to believe I'm almost anybody except Horatio Bristle." But he chuckled.

The sleigh jingled on through the keen darkness of Christmas Eve. Everything was quiet, now, and the stars shone among the bare trees. Someone began to sing, very softly. "Silent Night . . . Holy Night . . ."

Bobo couldn't be sure, but it certainly sounded like Jane Burke.

•

Edith Ballinger Price (1897–1997), poet, short-story writer, and novelist, wrote during the first half of the twentieth century. She was instrumental in starting the Brownie Girl Scouts program in the United States.

THE REAL CHRISTMAS SPIRIT

HELEN E. RICHARDS

Sis and James, Jr., hadn't realized times were so tough for the Davenport family—not until they overheard their parents worrying about how they were going to get through Christmas without losing face with their neighbors.

Sis and James looked at each other in dismay. . . . Finally they decided it was up to them to save the day.

In a prosperous, Middle Western town, on the east side, at the upper end of a long avenue of comfortable homes, the street veers suddenly to the right and ends in Cedar Hill, a blind, but beautiful alley, bordered with lawns, decorated at this time of year with strange figures of gunny sacking wound with cord and with piles of straw overlaid with boards. Back of these suggestions of the landscape gardener stand four houses, wide-spreading, luxurious—Cedar Hill homes of the Davenports, the Clydes, the Lees, and the Ludingtons.

On Christmas Eve it was the custom for Cordelia Davenport to give a recital, and the Clydes and the Lees and the Ludingtons came laden with their articles of commerce, and hung them on the Davenport Christmas tree at the end of a long drawingroom. The little group of families on Cedar Hill always celebrated royally, because it was within the power of Cedar Hill residents to do so.

"And Cedar Hill leads the town," quoted James Davenport, Jr., to his sister.

James, Jr., was taller than his father, and he carried himself with a regal air in spite of his extreme youth. He drew down the library shades, and flung himself into an armchair.

"Sis, what do you say to going to Meredith's for programs? They have some gorgeous new leather things. I say white morocco, with the Davenport coat of arms in gold and blue. How does that strike you?"

"And mistletoe instead of holly. Bort's is taking orders now," supplemented Sis. "And I want mother to try that new caterer on West Fifth. They say he is so much better than—" She stopped suddenly, and looked up at James with a startled expression. Both listened intently. They heard the voice of their mother talking to James, Sr., in the music room.

"It isn't right, James, with all the financial reverses you have suffered this year and all the calls there are for charity, that we should spend so lavishly. I shall never forget how nearly we came to losing the old home itself. We ought not to have any recital at all!"

"No recital!" James, Sr., gasped. "What will the Ludingtons say?" he cried.

"The Ludingtons can be thankful that they live in well-favored America, and not in starving Germany."

James, Jr., slipped from his chair and caught his sister's arm.

"What is it?" he whispered. "What are they talking about?"

"Hush!"

James, Sr., was speaking again. "We can manage the recital," I think, Cordelia, and have something to give besides," he said in a low, generous voice.

"Then we ought to give twice as much, and go without the recital," insisted Mrs. Davenport. "It would be positively wicked for us to have the usual orgy of presents and feasting while there is such great need. The Davenports have always led. Let us lead now, in giving—in sacrifice."

"What will the children say?" asked her husband, suddenly.

"Never mind what they say, James. They need just this kind of experience. They are spendthrifts, both of them. Jim, Jr., hasn't the first notion of the value of money, and as for Sis—we've encouraged her in—oh, well, never mind. We always had more than enough, until the stock company failed. Perhaps it hasn't been best not to let them know about our worries," she added thoughtfully.

Sis gazed at her brother solemnly. "Are we that bad, Jim?" she questioned under her breath.

He was silent. The fire in the grate crackled and snapped and leaped and fell. The voices in the music-room had dropped to a lower key.

"What about stock failing?" James, Jr., asked finally. "I heard rumors at college, but I didn't suppose it was really so, when Dad didn't mention anything."

James, Jr., slung himself forward, resting his chin in his hands. Sis watched him in silence.

"We'll let the morocco programs go—eh, Sis?" he laughed shortly. Then he looked up. "See here—how much money have you?"

"Not more than five dollars, I guess. I spent the rest for—"

"And I haven't a cent!"

Sis gazed at him tremulously. "We can't have any Christmas," she faltered.

James, Jr., stood up. In the firelight, against the dark background of the library, he loomed like a young giant, his features standing out white, vivid, forceful, with all the Davenport pride and reserve. Quietly he put his hands in his pockets and stared into the fire.

"We have always led, Sis, as Mother says," he said slowly; "and our house has always been gay at Christmas time. We have to keep it up!"

"But the money, Jim—if we—"

"We can celebrate Christmas without money, Sis. What's family pride for? It isn't money pride, Sis, it's the real article. We'll have our party just the same. And we'll do it on what money we can scare up between us!"

The time had been, years before, when the Cedar Hill families were poor, when the Davenport Christmas party had been very gay, but very economical. But of late years, money and social rivalry had increased the expenditure and stunted the gaiety. Cordelia Davenport had been the leader, and if sometimes she sighed for more sincerity and less show in their social affairs, still it had not occurred to her that the situation could be remedied. So used had she become to professional singers and high-priced caterers, that to forego these luxuries, even from a sense of duty, meant no Christmas festivity, and she sighed as she thought how they would miss the annual gathering.

James, Sr., too, much as he hated the stately social functions, began to realize a loss as the holidays approached.

"No Christmas this year," he said with a shrug as he met Mr. Clyde at the corner and they turned toward Cedar Hill for dinner.

"That's all right," declared Clyde, seriously. "We're cutting out some things, too. Rather hard on the children."

Silently the two men strode on up the hill, and it did not occur to either of them that they could celebrate without an outlay.

"What can you do without money?" asked Davenport, gloomily.

"I know," nodded Clyde. "It doesn't rain Christmas doings—you have to buy them."

It was a few days before Christmas, and Cordelia Davenport was making her afternoon toilet before a tall mirror in her dressing room. Tall mirrors were rather a specialty with her, and if any one of her family wished to give her an expensive present, he knew without asking that she could find space somewhere for another mirror—or for a cut-glass candlestick. She was not sure which of these she liked best. James, Jr., once said that his mother ought to live in a glass house.

Today, as Mrs. Davenport dressed, she saw reflected in her mirror the figure of a woman crossing the street and aiming straight for her front door. It was a portly figure, increased to absurdity by a huge collaret and a muff the size of two Angora cats.

"Madam Ludington!" exclaimed Cordelia; "what can she possibly want?"

This question did not imply that Madam's calls were infrequent, but merely that her movements were sometimes social maneuvers. The recent stricture in the Christmas expenditure of the Davenports altered the social opportunities.

"It is so lovely of you to have us just the same as ever," Madam greeted Mrs. Davenport sincerely and cordially, "just lovely! It's the true Christmas spirit. You don't know how we all appreciate it."

Cordelia Davenport smiled vaguely. Was this sarcasm? She remembered uncomfortably the costly present she had received from Madam a year ago.

"Yes?" she parried pleasantly.

"And the invitations are too delightful. So informal. I told Sis I hoped she would always come hereafter to deliver them—she is growing into a very charming young lady."

"Yes," Cordelia assented, "I'm very proud of my girl—she is so trustworthy."

What had Sis done? What had happened? But Sis WAS trustworthy. Mrs. Davenport said it over and over frantically to herself while she smiled at her guest.

"We are all so delighted with your idea of entertaining us simply. It is so different!"

Madam Ludington's good faith was evident, but Cordelia could scarcely appreciate it—she was too much alarmed.

"I think," she said with sudden inspiration, and she marveled at herself as she said it, "that a merry Christmas is not dependent on a bank account."

The plump, shrewd face of her neighbor lighted suddenly. "But we had forgotten that!" she exclaimed.

When James, Sr., came home for dinner, he was unusually gay. His wife told him of Madam Ludington's visit.

"Trust the Davenports for upholding the family honor," he laughed easily; "they've never failed yet, and they never will. James, Jr., and Sis came into the office this afternoon and told me they were going to entertain the usual crowd on five dollars. What do you think of that? Sis said she would bake four dozen cookies after some recipe she learned at school."

Cordelia stared.

"Four dozen cookies!" she cried. "They aren't expecting to feed Madam Ludington and the rest on COOKIES?"

James, Sr., looked alarmed. This appalling deduction had not occurred to him. But relief at the attitude of his son and daughter had made him feel light-hearted.

"Well, perhaps that isn't enough," he returned quickly; "Madam is a hearty eater." Then they both laughed till they cried.

"It will be perfectly awful," she sobbed, "to give those people cookies, but the children mean well!"

Then she dried her eyes and went to arrange her hair. But she stopped short in astonishment.

"James!" she called. "James, come here!"

Before them, where the long broad mirror had hung, was a plain bare wall, and near the center, in an inadequate attempt to fill the space, hung James, Sr.'s, shaving-glass. Stuck to the wall with a pin was a bit of paper scrawled in the handwriting of Jim, Jr. "Merry Christmas, folks!" it challenged. They were disarmed. There was nothing to do but laugh and wonder. The little paper as much as said: "Don't ask any questions."

James, Sr., was silent for a space.

"Cordelia," he said finally, "we've grown away—far away from the old simple good times. Perhaps the children can bring us back. Let's not worry about their plans. We can trust them. Let's be game."

Mrs. Davenport gazed at him contemplatively, a slight smile beginning to curl about the corners of her mouth.

"Why—" she hesitated, "why—perhaps you're right."

That night, when James, Sr., came downstairs to dinner, he tripped on an innocent-looking yellow bag which stood on the lower step. By an agile leap he saved his life and landed on the rug, while a little stream of lemons rolled gaily across the polished floor.

"There!" muttered Jim, Jr., to Sis in the dining room; "I forgot to take away that bag."

A new faction had arisen at Cedar Hill, eager, inventive, at work for the preservation of a nearly lost holiday. All that Merry Christmas had meant, all that it had failed to mean because of worldliness and social bickerings, hovered fantastically before the residents of Cedar Hill. Secrecy met them at every turn. As the days passed on, the atmosphere became charged to its utmost with a current of mystery such as Merry Christmas had not brought for years.

On Christmas Eve there was a final rendezvous in the Davenport drawing room—a flurried, joyous bunch of fourteen Cedar Hill young folks, whom James and Sis had pressed into service for the occasion.

They ranged in age from the youngest Ludington—a five-year-old wee mannie in curls and kilts—to the Lee twins, just of age and decked in swallow-tails and white shirt fronts. James, Jr., who had passed his twentieth birthday and overtopped the Lees by two inches, was master of ceremonies, and led proceedings in his gravely dignified way. Next to him was Isabelle Clyde, the tall blonde, beautiful in blue chiffon, and then Sis—black-crowned Sis, whose graceful ways and glorious blue-black hair were attractions which made one forget the color of her gown.

Hastily they stationed themselves in the front hall, the Lee twins, butler-wise at either side of the drawing room entrance ready to pull the curtains; James, Jr., and Sis waiting to receive, and the rest hustling to the place allotted to them, to tune their various instruments. There was indeed an orchestra. It consisted of one piano, one violin, four ukuleles, and three combs, well papered, well tuned.

What a travesty on the usual Davenport recital! Will the proud Cedar Hillites be game? Is the contrast too great? Is it indeed true that it does not rain Christmas festivities—that we must buy them? At this moment Sis turned an appealing glance toward James, Jr. Did he, too, feel the inadequacy of their attempt? But her brother's eyes were fixed toward the top of the carved oak staircase where his mother and father were descending, evidently determined to be game whatever the cost, and smilingly concealing any misgivings.

As they reached the hall below, Cordelia glanced at the floor. The rugs were gone, and from the big front door stretched a strip of canvas, fastened carefully with thumb tacks.

"What's this for?" she asked in surprise, turning to her son.

"We don't know, mother," James, Jr., told her with a grin. "Mr. Lee asked us to put it down."

"Mr. Lee!"

At that instant sounded a lugubrious thud on the front porch, followed by shouts of laughter. The door burst open, and in rushed Mr. Lee, Mr. Ludington, Mr. Clyde, and all the other guests, dragging a heavy weight across the mysterious canvas.

"Hello, Davenport! Got a place for this thing?"

"Oh, oh, a Yule log!" "All decorated with holly—how perfectly lovely!" "Wait, I'll help!"

Pushing and laughing, the orchestra piled into the hall to see.

"It ought to have come at sundown," explained Clyde; "but the invitation said eight o'clock, so—" he gave a final heave, and the huge thing settled into place, and the festive fire was lighted.

Never had the Davenport Christmas entertainment started in so unceremonious a fashion. The company stood about talking excitedly, and not till the old Yule log was actually beginning to kindle, did they go upstairs to remove their wraps.

Cordelia turned to Sis and James, Jr. "It's going to be perfectly splendid!" she said under her breath. "Your father and I almost worried, but they are taking it beautifully."

The music had begun—the violin wailed, the combs buzzed. Sis seized her mother's arm and pointed. Cordelia Davenport gasped. Down the staircase came Mr. and Mrs. Lee arm in arm in solemnity unequaled, and behind them trooped the other guests, all arrayed in costumes the splendor of which no Davenport recital had ever witnessed. Mrs. Lee's gown was composed completely of ruffles from the Sunday comic section, in pink and red and blue. Her husband was in black and white, as became a gentleman, with narrow spiral ruffles of the *Daily Tribune* and the *Argus-Herald* incasing each leg and arm.

Were they game? Could anything in all the great town, with its wealth and pride, its poverty and greater pride, its struggles and sorrows, its jealousies and joys, equal the true Christmas spirit of haughty grandmother Ludington in her rustling gown of fine print "want ads"?

The youngest Ludington jumped before her and clapped his hands and cried, "O Gamma! Gamma!" and jumped again and lost his balance on the waxed floor, and had to be hugged and comforted.

The orchestra trembled and squeaked, and failed in laughter. The guests rustled and swished and laughed, while the Lee twins, faithful to their office, drew back the heavy crimson portieres and revealed the Christmas drawing room. There were no festoons of ground pine, no holly wreaths, not even the ancient bunch of mistletoe—but a blaze of glory that dazzled and blinded. The walls were lined with plate-glass mirrors, full length, expansive, reflecting and reflecting in bewildering infinity, multiplying a thousandfold the candles burning in Cordelia Davenport's cut-glass candlesticks. There was the big library mirror, with its gilded frame, the mirrors from diningroom, hall, and guestrooms, and all the family looking-glasses—everything that would reflect. And in the center of the room, upon a tiny table, stood a diminutive Davenport Christmas tree, its tiny candles glittering and winking at their million reproductions reflected on every side. There were fifty Christmas trees—there were hundreds—thousands, it seemed! There were twenty-five guests—there were fifty—there were a hundred!

And then the recital began with an opening chorus by the Cedar Hill, Jr., fourteen—a quaint old Christmas carol they had learned at school.

After the singing was over, Ludington turned to James, Sr.

"This is great!" he cried. "Why didn't we ever do it before? What's this, Sis? Going to give these to me?" he went on comically. She had paused before him with a silver tray of tiny cards.

Sis laughed. "No, sir. You may have just one. We're going to set you all to work. The card will tell you what to do."

"Number four! Number four! Where's number four?" called Archie Clyde, rushing frantically about.

"O Isabelle, are you seven? You and I are to beat the eggs!"

"Number four—number four!"

James, Sr., roused. "What's all this about? Why, I'm number four—my card is marked four. Here, Archie, what do you want?"

The boy poised on one leg in front of him, and read from his card: "Help number four turn the freezers."

"'When the gong sounds, lead the way to the kitchen,'" read Mrs. Lee, meditatively. "Why—where IS the kitchen?"

Madam Ludington was adjusting her eyeglasses. "Here, somebody," she cried; "do read my card for me!" She handed it to a curly-headed Ludington.

"O Grandma! You are to cut the cake! Oh, isn't this fun? Wait—I'll tell you what it says. 'Please cut the cake which you will find on the broad shelf in the serving-room. There is a knife in the left-hand upper drawer of the kitchen cabinet.'"

"Oh," cried Madam, 'how can I ever do anything in these paper furbelows?"

A gong sounded above the din. "Come on, everybody," called Mrs. Lee; "we're going to the kitchen!"

"The freezers are all packed—all you have to do is keep them rolling," explained James, Sr., to Archie, after an examination of the two rounded tubs which seemed screwed to the table.

"Where's the egg beater? Where's the—"

"Doesn't it tell? Why, yes! 'On hanger above the sink'—here it is!"

Such laughter, such informality, never had been known. The newspapered guests flew back and forth. They folded paper napkins, they arranged plates of cookies, they beat eggs, and turned them stiff and foaming into the lemon sherbet. They carried chairs, they drew water and filled glasses.

"I'm to light the candles on the cake," sang Mrs. Clyde; 'but where are the matches?"

"Here—here—in this tin box!"

At last all was ready, and the company returned to the Christmas drawing-room to eat what they themselves had prepared and served.

"You see, we couldn't have a caterer," Sis explained.

"Ladies and gentlemen!" the voice of James, Jr., rose above the din, and they looked to where he stood, straight and tall, between the bay windows. "Ladies and gentlemen. Twenty-five years ago tonight, on Cedar Hill, in the Davenport parlor, nine persons gathered to celebrate Christmas Eve. On that night a compact was made in the light of the Christmas candles to the effect that so long as they were neighbors, in sickness, or in health, in adversity as well as prosperity, they would, unless unavoidably prevented, spend each ensuing Christmas night together. Those nine persons were Mr. and Mrs. Frank Clyde, Mr. and Mrs. Walter Lee, Mr. and Mrs. Eugene Ludington, Madam Ludington, and Mr. and Mrs. James Davenport. Wherefore we, the children and heirs of the aforesaid persons, have determined that, so long as the power within us lies, we will, with sincerity and good will to all, aid and abet the aforesaid persons, and if at any time their courage fails, or money is otherwise diverted, we will, by reason of our inherited ability and traditional inventiveness, provide such entertainment as may be needed for the annual occasion. In token whereof we present you with this birthday cake, holding twenty-five candles, each one of which represents a single Christmas celebration during the past quarter century. And," he added with a grin, "as there are now twenty-five of us, including two guests, there is just one piece apiece, with a candle for each!"

Cordelia Davenport's eyes glowed. She turned to her daughter.

"O Sis!" she breathed, "how did you know? Who told you?"

"Madam Ludington. And oh Mother, she's been just the best help! She suggested the paper costumes, too. Do look at her!"

The old lady was shaking with laughter, while she tried to repair a damaged paper flounce with pins.

And then, at last, amid the clamor of tongues there sounded distant sweet chords. Intrigued, the guests sought the source. In the music room the youngest Ludington, the little mannie in curls and kilts, stood by the grand piano looking at Sis. All the lanterns and candles but one had been extinguished. There was a sudden hush.

Sis played the opening chord of Martin Luther's beloved children's hymn, then the child turned and began to sing:

> *"Away in a manger, no crib for a bed,*
> *The little Lord Jesus laid down His sweet head.*
> *The stars in the bright sky looked down where He lay,*
> *The little Lord Jesus asleep on the hay!"*

Across the room where the singer gazed as he sang . . . was a crèche, illuminated by three candles. As the last notes died away into the night, there followed absolute silence.

Christ had returned to Cedar Hill Christmas.

•

Helen E. Richards wrote for popular and inspirational magazines during the first half of the twentieth century.

Christmas Memories

A TREE FOR BENJI

HAROLD IVAN SMITH

Why was his father so bullheaded in his refusal to permit a Christmas tree in his house? It just didn't make sense. And now to break little Benji's heart!

He decided to have it out with his father, once and for all.

John Stevens rubbed his eyes as he stretched on the old couch in the living room. Today was December 21. Christmas was only four days away. Time was running out. How many times had eight-year-old Benji, his son, impatiently demanded, "When are we going to put up the tree?"

How could he tell him there wasn't going to be a tree this year? Last year—and the years before that—there had been a marriage, a reason to celebrate. Now . . . nothing. But that wasn't the real reason. There was that strange attitude of his dad, Benji's grandfather.

Eight months ago John had given up and moved in with his parents. Somehow, trying to pay the bills, care for the three boys, be father and mother, and deal with the gnawing hurt from the divorce demanded too much energy.

The old farm house, however, was over-crowded. His boys shared the tiny bedroom he had once shared with three brothers, and John longed for a bedroom now more than he had as a child.

Well, at least they were together. His mind went to Benji—the youngest child, the only one who kept talking about Jesus, and how He could do the impossible. Must have gotten that from some Sunday School. It certainly didn't run in the family. And how was Benji really dealing with the divorce? How many times had he asked about that tree?

John heard his father's telltale footsteps in the kitchen. The morning routine had not changed in decades. By the time John rolled out from under the covers, the coffee would be ready. Perhaps this was the morning to confront the old man about the tree.

He swung off the couch and shuffled into the kitchen.

"Morning," he said. His dad turned from the stove as though surprised to see him.

"Morning! Want some coffee?"

"Yeah, I better." John stretched again as he sat down to the same scarred table at which he had eaten almost every meal in his childhood. His dad placed a cup of steaming coffee in front of him, then slid the sugar and cream across the table.

"What's up today?" John asked.

"Thought I'd mend that fence." John noticed that his father assumed he knew which section. John pressed on.

"Soon be Christmas." The old man did not respond. John quickly took another sip of coffee, seeking courage.

"Benji keeps asking when we're going to put up that tree. I don't know what to tell him."

A long silence followed. The old man drained the last of his coffee and stared at the bottom of his mug.

"Dad?" John pleaded.

"Ever been a tree that you can remember?" the old man said, jerking his gaze from the mug to his son.

"No, Dad." And that's just it . . ." Abruptly, the elder Stevens stood and moved without effort to the sink. He placed the mug on the drainboard and left the room.

John could not remember a Christmas tree in this house. For that reason, on the first Christmas of his marriage, he had squeezed the biggest tree he could find into their tiny apartment, mostly to spite the old man. His father had not even commented on it.

Why was his dad so against a Christmas tree? John knew some people had religious objections, but his dad wasn't fond of churches.

He had not heard his mother's footsteps.

"Morning, son," she mumbled. "Radio says it's 14 degrees outside. When you leave for work, be sure and bundle up." She reached for her coffee mug and poured the coffee. Then she joined her son at the table. "How did you sleep?"

"Fine." That reply stretched the truth, but John didn't want to add another worry to his mom's overload.

"I'm concerned about your back, son . . ." John cut into the conversation, recycled from other mornings.

"Well, I've got more things than my back to worry 'bout." John stepped to the stove to pour another cup.

"Like Benji?" his mom asked.

"What about Benji? Has he been giving you problems?"

"That little guy's never a problem. But he sure is wanting a tree. That's all he talked about yesterday after he got home from school. A tree!"

"Well, I don't want him pestering you . . ."

His mother cut him off. "Grandmothers delight in being pestered. He tells me most things on his mind. Eight-year-olds can't store much in their silos." She gestured toward her head. John moved his chair closer to his mother's.

"Mom, why hasn't there been a Christmas tree in this house?"

Before she spoke, his mother stroked a rough place on the table top. Then she said, "You asked me Benji's question every Christmas until you were ten." Her voice conveyed no trace of annoyance. "Funny . . . Benji is so much like you . . . takes me back. He's the spitting image of you." John could not be certain if his mother were stalling or merely avoiding the question.

"Mom, why isn't there a *tree*?" John tried to keep the desperation from his voice.

"Same answer now as then. Just, 'cause."

"That's no answer for Benji. He's smart."

John's mother looked away, her eyes brimming. "Then I don't know! I never remember a tree, and I've lived in this house for 40 years. Your dad don't like questions when he makes up his mind on something!"

"Did you ever ask him?"

"Once."

"What did he say?"

"Nothing. He just sat there in that rocking chair of his and stared at the wall."

John would have pressed the subject but chimes from the old clock on the fireplace mantle drifted in to the kitchen, reminding him he was late. The questions would have to wait.

Ten hours later, John pulled off the paved road and onto the gravel road that led to the farmhouse. He was exhausted from another day at the plant. Abruptly, Benji and his old mangy dog darted into his path. John stopped the car and rolled down the window.

"Been waiting for you," Benji said. "Wanna show you something." John took his foot off the brake and the car started. "No, Dad. I want to show you something!" Benji pleaded.

"What?" John snapped.

"Come on." Benji turned and bolted toward the woods. His dog barked once and followed. John turned the motor off and climbed out of the car. A blast of cold wind stung him. Whatever Benji wanted him to see must be important to risk this wind. Fortunately, Benji didn't run far.

"There it is." John couldn't follow his gesture.

"What, Benji?" he demanded impatiently.

"That's the one . . . that's the tree I want Granddad to put up for Christmas." The impact of the words were as raw as the December wind. "It's just right!" Benji proudly stated. John looked at a tree that would cost about $25 in the city.

"Well, we'll have to think about it." The sentence escaped John before he considered its impact. He angrily kicked a frozen clod of dirt. Why not tell Benji the truth? There wasn't going to be a tree. He turned and walked rapidly toward the car.

"Dad?" Benji protested.

"Come on. Let's go. Grandma's got supper waiting." The little fellow turned for one last look at the tree.

They drove to the house in silence. If only Benji knew how many trees John had picked out before he quit trying to change his dad's mind.

John looked at his son huddled against the passenger door.

"What's wrong, pardner?"

"Nothing." But John recognized the hurt. Benji opened the door and ran toward the house.

John slammed his hand against the steering wheel, more from frustration than anger. Now, he'd have to confront his dad in a way no son should.

The house was again silent; the boys asleep. The three adults had silently watched TV. As the theme song of the late news announced the hour, John's father stood and remarked, "Getting late," his equivalent of "Good night."

"Dad, I need to talk to you . . ." The old man switched off the TV. "Dad, Benji is wanting a Christmas tree. He's been through so much. And, well, I know this is your house and we're guests here, but how do I tell an eight-year-old, 'no tree'?"

There was a long silence. John couldn't be sure his mother was still in the room.

"Tell him there's never been a tree." The old man retorted too sharply for John's comfort. But still John thought he sensed a softening. He pressed on.

"He'll want to know why."

Another silence—this one longer. Then his father spoke slowly. "I was Benji's age. We'd gone down to the Perkins' place and cut the tree I'd picked out. It was a beauty. Back then we owned all that land. Pulled that tree home and put it up right there in that corner." He pointed toward the stairwell.

"We didn't have ornaments like most folk. Just popcorn strings and some ribbons. But it was pretty enough. My momma helped us string that popcorn and told us Christmas stories." The old man stopped. Only the ticking of the mantle clock broke the silence.

"Momma," the old man stopped again and cleared his throat. "Momma died that next day. Hadn't even been sick. She was the one who had trusted Jesus, and she was the one who died. I couldn't understand it all."

John edged forward on the couch because his father's words were whispered. "We didn't have funeral homes around here then. People were laid out at home. So, we had to take down the tree to put her casket there."

Suddenly, John's heart intertwined with his dad's. *How could an eight-year-old deal with that ugly invasion?* He saw his mother's tear-filled eyes dart from him to her husband.

"My momma was buried on Christmas Day . . . and I've never felt like celebrating."

After a moment John spoke, carefully struggling for words. "Dad, why didn't you tell me before now?"

"Every Christmas comes, I think about it. Can't seem to get it out of my mind," he said in his usual evasive way. Then the clock struck the half hour. As if on signal, the old man looked at the clock, then resumed his stoic posture. "Getting late," he said as he shuffled out of the room.

If John expected a comment from his mother, he was disappointed. "Turn out the lights, John, when you go to bed." But her words were spoken softly.

Later, in the darkened room, John sat listening to the systematic tick-tick of the mantle clock. He turned to confront it. The clock had been a gift for his grandparents on their wedding day. How many other memories of that woman remained in this farmhouse to tease the eight-year-old child that cowered within the toughness of the 69-year-old-farmer-father?

Finally, he punched the pillows in his nightly ritual. Tomorrow was December 23. Somehow he'd have to find a way to explain this to Benji. Although he didn't know much about the Bible, perhaps he could tie it into the Christmas story. Wasn't there something about a tree symbolizing eternal life? And Benji's great grandmother had evidently been a believer. John turned restlessly, trying to fit the pieces together.

A few feet away behind the security of the white bedroom door, tears trickled down the old man's face and wet the pillowcase. Sally Stevens had slept with this man for 50 years and had never seen a mood like this one. She called his name, but there was no response.

The next afternoon, as Benji raced down the front steps of Martin Elementary School he was greeted by a different horn. He discovered his granddad's old, exhausted '53 truck.

"Hi, Granddad," he said as he got in and pulled the rickety old door shut. The old man started the tired engine, and pulled away from the curb.

"Have a good day, Boy?" the old man asked. Benji recited what a great time they had had this last day of school before the Christmas break. The truck sputtered along old bumpy roads heading home. When they turned down the lane leading to the woods, no explanation was offered or requested.

"See all that land over there, Boy?" the old man asked. "My daddy, your granddaddy, used to own all this. When I was your age I'd come down here and fight Indians." His voice gave the threat of danger.

"*Real* Indians?" Benji asked, his eyes the size of half-dollars. The old man laughed.

"No, Boy. Pretend Indians. This was my favorite place in the whole world." He pulled off the road and hopped out of the truck.

"Boy, you see that tree?" he raised his arm to identify a tall tree in a slump. Benji whispered, "Yes, sir."

"When I was your age I wanted to chop down that tree and take it home."

"But, Granddad, wasn't it awfully big to take home?"

"Ah, Boy," he said with a laugh. "It wasn't that big *then* . . . it was like, well, that one over there." Benji's eyes followed the old man's gesture to the very tree he had picked out the other day.

"Granddad," he exclaimed, "that would sure make a pretty Christmas tree!" After a moment he added, "Wouldn't it?"

From deep within the old man's spirit, the voice that responded was not that tarnished by years of denial, but an eight-year-old boy's.

"Sure would, Boy. Sure would! Go get the ax . . . in the truck."

The old man swung the ax with the skill of years. One more solid swing of the ax would topple the cedar tree. The old man stopped. "Put out your hands, Boy." Benji complied. "Here, you bring her down." Benji started to question. "You can do it—*your own Christmas tree.*"

Benji's eyes widened. His mind spun. *Imagine, cutting his own Christmas tree . . . no one else in his school could do that!*

Benji swung the ax. The tree swayed, and fell slowly to the ground. Benji squealed with glee.

"Good job, Boy. Good job!"

John knew what he would say—or at least what he *thought* he would tell Benji. For ten miles he had carefully rehearsed his lines. Hopefully, he had anticipated every question Benji would ask.

He got out of his car and walked toward the porch. Taking a deep breath, he opened the screen door and turned the old porcelain knob. His first thoughts were that he was in the wrong house. There stood a huge cedar tree filling the corner where he imagined another tree had once stood.

John looked to the old man for a word of explanation.

"Boy picked out a good one, didn't he?"

In that moment, father and son spoke a new language. Benji stared at them only a moment. Then he returned to hanging the ornaments his grandmother handed him.

"It's a tree for Benji," the old man said brightly, although his chin wobbled. "For Benji."

Then the final tears of a long season fell from the eyes of a 69-year-old man who, as a boy, had also been called Benji.

•

Harold Ivan Smith wrote for inspirational magazines during the second half of the twentieth century.

THE RED ENVELOPE

NANCY N. RUE

Tom was gone. How could she possibly face Christmas without him? Worse yet, the children were all acting as if it were Christmas as usual.

How could they!

Slice. Scoop. Plop.
I don't feel like doing this.
Slice. Scoop. Plop.
I don't want to do this. I don't want to shop—
Slice. Scoop. Plop.
I don't want to decorate. I just want to skip it—
Slice. Scoop. Plop.
And pretend I didn't notice this year.

I sliced, scooped, and plopped the last of the dough from the ready-made cookie dough package and shoved the cookie sheet into the oven. They were a far cry from the bejeweled affairs I'd baked for twenty-six years, and the only reason I'd even summoned up the effort to throw these on a pan was because Ben had opened and re-opened the cookie jar four times the previous night before saying with fourteen-year-old tact, "What—you're not baking this year? What's up with that?"

He'd gone on to inform me that tomorrow—now today—was the twenty-third and that Ginger and Paul would be arriving in two days, and they were going to "freak" when there wasn't any "cool stuff to eat like usual." This from the same kid who flipped the channel every time a holiday commercial came on and had for years been eschewing all talk of a family photo for the annual Christmas card.

I hadn't even considered a family picture this year. A big piece of the family was now missing—or hadn't anybody noticed?

All my friends had been telling me practically since the day of the funeral, "Michelle, the first year after you lose your husband is the hardest. You have to go through the first Valentine's Day without him, the first birthday, the first anniversary—"

They hadn't been kidding. What they hadn't told me was that Christmas was going to surpass all of them in hard-to-take. It wasn't that Ken had loved Christmas that much. He was as bad as Ben and Scrooge put together when it came to holiday advertisements—said the whole thing was too commercial and that when you really thought about it Easter was a much more important celebration in the church.

I flopped down on a stool at the kitchen counter and half-heartedly started a list of who I needed to buy for. Ginger had called last night—right after Ben's fifth trip to the empty cookie receptacle—giggling and shushing the dormitory howls behind her.

"I just finished my last final!" she shrieked into the phone. "I'll be home day after tomorrow. Do you know what I'm looking forward to?"

"Sleeping for 72 straight hours?" I said.

"No." She'd sounded a little deflated. "Seeing all those presents piled up under the tree. I've never cared what was in them or how many were for me—I just like seeing them there. How weird is that?"

Not weird at all, my love, I thought now, as I penciled in Ben, Ginger, Paul, his wife Amy, my grandson Danny. *Just highly unlikely.*

I hadn't done any shopping. I couldn't even think about my tradition of wrapping every gift so that it was more a work of art on the outside than the article within. And there had been no way I could spend my usual three days decorating—two hours on the manger scene alone. But my kids were still expecting it—even Paul who at 25 had a child of his own, and still asked me last week when he called if I had the old John Denver Christmas album dusted off yet.

I snapped the pencil down on the counter. None of them seemed to even suspect that this wasn't going to be the usual Tabb family Christmas. They were all acting as if their father's death eleven months ago wasn't going to change a thing about our celebration. As far as I was concerned, there wasn't that much to deck the halls about. Ken was gone. I was empty and unmotivated and at best annoyed. At worst, I wished they'd all just open the presents and carve the turkey without me.

When the oven dinged, I piled two dozen plain brown circles on a plate and left a note for Ben: *I don't want to hear any more complaining! Gone shopping. I love you. Mom.*

The complaining, however, went on in my head as I elbowed my way through the mob at the mall.

Ken was right, I thought. *This is all a joke.*

It really was everything he hated—canned music droning its false merriment somewhere in the nebulous background—garish signs luring me to buy—squabbling, tired-looking families dragging themselves around, worrying about their credit card limits as they snapped at their children.

Funny, I thought, while gazing sightlessly at a display of earrings I knew neither Ginger nor Amy would wear, *all the time Ken was here pointing all this out to me, it never bothered me. Now it's all I can see.*

I abandoned the earring idea and took to wandering the mall, hoping for inspiration so Ginger would have something to look at under the tree. It wasn't going to be like years past—I should have told her that. She wasn't going to see the knee-deep collection of exquisitely wrapped treasures that Ken always shook his head over while he grinned at me.

"You've gone hog-wild again," he would always tell me, and then he would add his one contribution. Every year he spent months looking for just the right worthy cause. Instead of buying me a gift, he'd write a check in my name to them—be it the Muscular Dystrophy Association or a local church that needed a new roof—and put it in a red envelope and tuck it onto a branch of our Christmas tree.

"This'll last all year," he'd tell me. "Maybe even change someone's life."

I stopped in mid-mall, causing a pile-up of aggravated shoppers behind me.

Ken wasn't there, a fact that didn't seem to bother the rest of my family. But he could still be with me, maybe just a little, if his part of Christmas was.

It wasn't a big spark of Christmas spirit—but it was enough to ram me through Sears and Wal-Mart—and See's candies. Paul liked the cashew turtles. It was also enough to nudge me with the fact that I couldn't put the envelope on the tree if we didn't have a tree. They still had some left at Safeway—and their turkeys looked good, too.

The decorations weren't buried too deeply in the garage. I'd barely gotten them put away last year before Ken had his heart attack. I thought about that as I dragged in boxes and untangled lights. The American Heart Association—that was the ticket. I stopped and wrote a check and miraculously located a red envelope in my desk. It would look perfect on this branch—what else to put there—I didn't get candy canes for the tree this year—maybe I'd string some popcorn—

I was deep into decorating when Ben emerged from the kitchen.

"Where are the rest of the cookies?" he said.

"What do you mean, 'the rest'?" I said. "There are two dozen on that plate."

"Were," Ben said.

I rolled my eyes at him as I backed up to check out the tree. "I'll make some more," I said.

"Are you going to put thingies on the next batch?" he said.

When I finished setting up the manger scene, I checked the kitchen for "thingies."

But the next day—Christmas Eve—my spirits sagged again. There is no lonelier feeling than standing in the midst of one's family—squealing, vivacious college daughter; sweet, gentle daughter-in-law; handsome, successful quarter-century son;

wide-eyed, super-charged four-year-old grandson; and even an awkward teenager whose hugs are like wet shoelaces—and being keenly aware that someone is missing.

Everyone else seemed to be avoiding the subject.

"The tree is *gorgeous*, Mom," Ginger said. She knelt in front of it and began hauling gifts out of a shopping bag to add to my pile.

"I love what you did with the wrappings, Michelle," Amy said. "You're always so creative."

"I forgot to buy wrapping paper," I told her. "I *had* to use newspaper."

None of *them* had forgotten a thing. There was no sign of mourning—it was Christmas as usual. Ben and Paul sparred over whose stocking was whose and Danny picked all the M&M's out of the cookies before he ate them and Ginger picked up every present and shook it. I put on a valiant smile and wished they would all go to bed so we could get this over with.

I stayed up after the last of them and slid my red envelope out from under my desk blotter. The tree lights winked softly at me as I tucked it between a misshapen glittery angel Ginger had made in second grade and Ben's Baby's First Christmas ball.

"I guess they have to go on with their lives, Ken," I whispered. "But I wish you were here."

It occurred to me as I unplugged the lights and groped toward the stairs that they might feel a little ashamed in the morning when they realized what it was. Would there be some, "Oh, yeah—I remember he always did that—" and some gulping and some exchanging of sheepish looks?

I hoped so.

Danny was, of course, up before the paper carrier. I dragged myself into the kitchen and found it already smelling like a Seattle coffee house.

"This is what we drink at school," Ginger told me, and handed me a cup.

"Have they already started on the presents?" I said.

She shook her heard, and for the first time I noticed a twinkle in her eye that was unprecedented for this hour of the morning.

"What are you up to?" I said.

"It's not just me," she said.

"Mom!" Paul yelled from that direction. "Come on—I can only hold this kid off for so long!"

"Come see'm, Gramma!" Danny called. "Come see all these red things!"

"What's he talking about?" I said.

"You'll see," Ginger said.

What I saw at first was my family, perched on the couch like a row of deliciously guilty canaries. What I saw next was our Christmas tree, dotted with bright red envelopes.

"Man, it got crowded in here last night," Ben said. "I came down here about two o'clock and freaked Amy out."

"I almost called 911 when I came down," Paul said. "Till I saw it was Ginger and not some burglar."

I missed most of that. I was standing in front of the tree, touching each one of the five envelopes I hadn't put there.

"Open them, Mom," Ginger said. "This was always the best part of Christmas."

Paul chuckled. "I was afraid everybody had forgotten."

No one had. From Paul, there was a check for Big Brothers, for kids who have to grow up without dads. From Amy, to the church, where she best remembered her father-in-law. From Ginger, for the Committee to Aid Abused Women—"because Dad always treated you like a queen," she said. From Ben, a twenty-dollar bill for a local drug program for kids, "since Dad was all freaked out about me staying clean."

The last envelope was lumpy and it jingled. When I opened it a handful of change tumbled out.

"That's from me, Gramma," Danny said, little bow-mouth pursed importantly. "For lost dogs—you know, like that one me an' Grandpa rescued."

I shot Paul a question with my eyes.

"He brought it up himself," Paul said.

Amy groaned happily. "He remembered at five o'clock this morning."

I pulled all the envelopes against my chest and hugged them.

"You know what's weird?" Ginger said. "I feel like Daddy's right here with us."

"Yeah, that's pretty weird," Ben said.

"But true," Paul said. "I felt like he's been here this whole time. I thought I'd be all bummed out this Christmas—but I don't need to be."

"Well, Ken," Amy said. She held up her coffee mug. "Here's to you."

Mugs clinked. Laughter danced across the living room.

I began to think about carving that turkey.

•

Nancy N. Rue is a prolific novelist and short-story writer. She is also the author of the Christian Heritage historical fiction series published by Focus on the Family. She writes from her home in Lebanon, Tennessee.

AND YOU SHALL RECEIVE

LOUIS ARTHUR CUNNINGHAM

Each had—before the terrible war—asked for the other's love. And each had been denied. So why, when it was all over, did their hearts continue to yearn for the impossible?

This is one of the greatest Canadian love stories to come out of World War II.

He had vowed long ago that he was done with all sentiment, all that the cynic in him called "sweetness and light," all faith in woman, all belief in the ultimate justice of God—for a woman had let him down badly and God had let so many good men die. For what?

For this, perhaps, thought Kilmer now, on Christmas Eve, as he walked the streets, gay and crowded, of his own city, with war behind him, all its ugliness and its pain.

For this, perhaps, that children's eyes might shine with that heavenly light as they gazed on the color and beauty of the Christmas trees in the shop windows; for this, that men and women might meet and shake hands and kiss and be glad and say, "Merry Christmas—Many of them," and go smiling on their way; for this, that from the cathedral as he passed the glory of the "Adeste" might stream out as the choir practiced for the Midnight Mass—

No more faith in woman—yet he had in his wanderings, by some remaining tenderness, passed the house where she lived. He knew the place, the old Courtney house on Peel Street, where Jeff Courtney had taken her as a bride, where now she lived as his widow with his son, a child of four.

"Don't be a fool, Kilmer," he had told himself, passing the house on Peel Street, seeing the holly-wreaths with their red ribbons, on door and window. "Don't go back for more punishment. All that was between Alison Chanter and you ended five years ago in a garden by the Thames. You said goodbye; there wasn't any more, there never can be any more. Get out of this town now—go west, go anywhere, but never back to her. She left you in that garden; we had quarreled, yes, but still she left you thinking, *She'll come back. We love each other. We'll always love.* But she never did come back. She went home, back to Canada, and in less than a month was married to Jeff Courtney—Jeff who died a year afterwards in Iceland waters. There's nothing there for you, fool—nothing of the Alison who walked in these places with you long ago—"

Still he passed her house, slowly, and then trudged by the church and the convent-school at whose gates he had waited for her so many afternoons—Alison of the red curls and deep blue eyes and small fair form. "That was long ago," he muttered—"that was long ago, and in another land, and that girl—there's nothing of her now—"

Still he kept walking along the familiar streets, past the old familiar places—the common with its snow-piled walks, its frozen fountain, its huge Christmas tree around which, these nights, the carol-singers gathered. He stood among the crowd by the tree now in the winter dusk and the lights were popping out all around the common—blue, red, yellow, shimmering and shifting and turning the smoke-smeared snow into a white and sequined beauty. Then the lights on the great spruce bloomed out suddenly and the big star on its tip seemed to blaze up to the silent ones that watched above, and some of the harshness, some of the war-graven lines, seemed to melt from Ives Kilmer's face, and he smiled when the voices, as of angels, filled the night and the heavens with the sweeping beauty of the Westminster Carol—

> *"Voices we have heard on high*
> *Lightly singing o'er the plain,*
> *And the mountains in reply*
> *Echo back their joyous strain—*
> *Gloria in excelsis Deo!"*

Kilmer's look was good then and his tall, spare figure, in the unaccustomed gray suit and Burberry and soft gray hat, stood straight and shoulder-square amongst the crowd—and Alison Courtney, who had been Alison Chanter, seeing him then, clutched young Jeff's hand till he tried to withdraw it and in her heart a song awoke that had been dead a long, long time.

"It's Ives," she said softly, but it was as if she was telling it to the world and the heavens. "It's Ives Kilmer, young Jeff. He's home again. He's here—" And then her mouth quivered and shook and all the lights and the tree and the snow made only a blur and she seemed to stand afar off and see a girl who was Alison Chanter praying for a crumb of forgiveness, a crust of kindness, found herself absurdly saying Masefield's words—"The beggar with the saucer in his hand asks only a penny of the passing crowd—"

"He refused me the crumb, the crust, the penny," she found herself saying then. "I'm too proud to ask again. I humbled myself once before him, I practically begged him to marry me and I'd stay in England or go home, whatever he wished. It was the unconditional surrender of Alison—and he sat like a stone and never said a word—not one word of forgiveness for the quarrel we'd had a week before—nothing whatever of the thing I'd asked of him—a thing so against my pride that I could not even face him but stood behind his shoulder, there in the dusk of the garden. I hated him then, when after I'd told him I'd go home and marry Jeff, he still didn't try to keep me. But I can't hate him now—maybe I never really did. But I'm proud now, I'll never crawl to him again."

><+>•O•<+>≺

But her eyes were a glory when they met Kilmer's, and she was glad that when they moved together and met and gave hand to hand, it was in the shadows on the edge of the crowd.

"Welcome home, Ives," she said. "I could scarcely believe it was you. But then, nice things come with Christmas trees."

He didn't speak for a moment or so; just stood with her gray gloved hand in his big fingers, still brown and hard from the sun and mud of the Flemish fields. Then he said, "You're lovelier than you ever were, Alison—so lovely—" Then he fetched himself up, remembering old things, harsh things, and said, "This is your boy."

"Yes." Alison's voice had lost some of its warmth too. "This is young Jeff. Say hello to Captain Kilmer, Jeff. He's an old friend."

Big eyes looked earnestly up at Ives and a small voice piped hello, the eyes never wavering from Kilmer's face. Kilmer thought, *Darn it, why does he have to have eyes like that, soft and wistful as a young collie's—lost eyes. He has no father, no man in his life. And he might have been mine; we might have done together all the things I planned to do—fishing, hunting in the autumn woods, ice-boating, learning to live, both of us. . . . But he's not mine. She walked out on me without giving me another chance, and made a life of her own. Well, she has something left of hers, but there's nothing at all left of mine.*

"Eh?" He started. He had been hearing Alison's low, husky voice, but not the words it was saying.

She laughed and there was a sudden pain in his heart: no other woman ever laughed like that—a rare, sweet sound. "You were dreaming, Ives. You didn't hear a word I said. I asked you if you were home for good?"

"Home? Here—oh, no. I had a few things to attend to. I'm selling the house and then—"

"Where then, Ives?"

He shook his head. "I don't really know yet. I have no one of my own, you know—no one who cares what I do or where I go."

She winced a little. He knew it, but he didn't care. Once there had been so much, so very much between them. Through this same common they had walked, under the great maples and balm o' Gilead in summer, between the high-piled snow in winter. He had carried her books from school, so many days, and here one September night—the night before he left for college—in the moon-dappled shadow, he had kissed her and said, "You're mine, Alison—always mine," and she had answered, unhesitant, "Always yours, Ives." Then the years took them in turn to London, Alison to study, Ives soon afterwards to fight in a war—and in England the dream had ended. And you can't re-live a dream.

The choristers were singing an old Welsh carol now,

> *"Deck the halls with boughs of holly,*
> *Fa-la-la-la-la-la-la-la-la.*
> *Now's the season to be jolly,*
> *Fa-la-la-la-la-la-la-la-la!"*

They stood silent, not knowing what to say, feeling the uselessness of small talk, the hopelessness of anything more grave.

"It's time for us to go." There was no life in her voice. "I promised Jeff I'd bring him to hear the Christmas carols. We didn't have them through the war. There was no tree, no lights, on account of the blackout. He never heard them before. He thinks the choir boys are angels." She smiled at Ives and he smiled back boyishly: once he'd stood there with Alison and "trolled out the ancient carol."

"You're remembering, Ives."

"No—no, Alison—trying to forget. Those times don't seem real to me any more. Here for a little while tonight, maybe—but—"

"I know."

They walked through the common, along the gaily lighted streets, then into the darker, quieter ones. Young Jeff's steps lagged. He'd had quite a day—an interview with Santa Claus, visits to many Christmas trees, then hearing the angels sing. He was glad when the big man picked him up and perched him on a shoulder that was like a rock. He put his small arms around Ives Kilmer's neck. "I like you," he said sleepily. "My own father is dead."

Ives did not look at Alison; he saw the white of her teeth as they caught her lip. His own eyes felt funny and a lot of things stirred in him that he had sworn never again to let awaken—emotions that could do things to a man. He was glad when they turned into Peel Street and he saw the lights in the windows glowing soft and red out on the snow.

He set Jeff down firmly and took off his hat, holding out his hand to Alison. She looked at him piteously for a moment, then her mouth stiffened and her small shoulders squared under the silver racoon.

"Thank you, Ives. You'll—I'll be seeing you again. You won't come in—"

"Thank you, Alison. I'd better be on my way. It's been good seeing you, too, and your son. We'll meet again some day, I hope—"

She didn't answer. She took the little boy in her arms and carried him up the steps. Ives saw the door open and caught a glimpse of shiny wood and soft warm lights, then the door closed behind her, behind all he had ever loved or ever would love.

The street seemed bleak and the wind was sharp and searching. He had a wild impulse to dash up the steps and go in after her and take her in his arms and put his mouth against hers and stay that way forever. . . .

The impulse died. There was nothing in it. He was just kidding himself. Their roads had parted long ago; they hadn't really converged or, if so, only briefly.

He turned away. Under the street lamp his feet slowed to a stop. He looked back once more at the holly-wreathed windows and fell deeper into loneliness. He thought he saw the shadow of Alison there in the lighted pane. *Five years is too long,* he thought—*far too long. We can't pick up those lovely threads again—not with any hope of completing the pattern. It's been lost. Better not try at all.*

He went back to the hotel and ate a tasteless dinner and sat for a while dreaming, thinking that a hotel lobby on Christmas Eve was the loneliest place a lonely man could select. The emptiness of his life impressed itself deeper upon him; there was no warmth, no loving-kindness in it. He thought of friends who had joined the silent orders of monks, thought of how he'd pitied them; now he began to understand them.

Alison—Alison, he thought; *if I go back to her, if she'd have me again, there'd always be Jeff Courtney's ghost there with us and I'd never know that it was really love she gave me. No, she must have given her only real love to him. I'd be just another man to her—and once I loved her. Once? I love her now more than I ever did.*

Midnight found him again walking the streets of the town, mingling with the current of people bound for church, thinking of the many Christmas Eves he had known, of Midnight Mass in the catacombs of Rome, in the little town of Bethlehem. The air was still, frosty; the stars never so bright in the deep blue sky, the Aurora played its spotlights on the world.

At the Cathedral door he hesitated, listening to the prelude to "Messa Angelorum," the "Mass of the Angels."

"Ah, well!" he muttered. "Once more—I'll go once more. After all, it's Christmas."

He went up the side aisle to the pew Kilmers had sat in for generations. He entered it and knelt and, as of old, turned his head to the transept, to the pew directly across the aisle—and saw her kneeling there, a blue halo hat crowning her dark red hair, framing a face that was to him always a madonna's face.

Her eyes strayed from the altar and met his briefly and her full lips curved a very little, then moved again in prayer. "Dear God!" she prayed. "Send Ives back to me. Don't let him go away. I need him. I always needed him. I'm so alone now, and my pride is gone. Bring him back to me. Bring him back to me."

Through the glory of the mass she prayed, thinking of the words, "Ask, and you shall receive." She had never asked much for herself. Pride and pique had driven her into a marriage which was not what she would have had with Kilmer. "I love him"—and it was a prayer. "God, I love him. Send him back to me."

The crowds streamed out of the church. Ives was at her shoulder, his hand upon her arm. In the shadow of the great buttress, he took her in his arms and kissed her and said, "Merry Christmas, Alison. Merry Christmas, my own, my own."

Her mouth trembled under his kiss and her arms were tight about his neck. Then he released her and they walked home through the silent streets, saying nothing, happy in each other, in their hearts a wondrous peace.

"You'll let me come in with you?" he said when they reached her house.

She only smiled at him and clung to his hand. They went in and stood before the fire in the living-room, looking down at the embers. Outside the wind made a weird keening and the town clock chimed out the half hour after one.

He drew her close to him, looking down at the shadowed planes of her face. "So you *do* love me, Alison—you *do* want me back," he said softly.

"How can you be so sure, Ives?"

"I heard you asking God to send me back to you."

She drew slowly away from him. "You—you heard me."

"There in the church tonight."

"You heard me when I was praying—you *couldn't* have. You—why, you couldn't hear me the night in the garden in England when I asked you aloud, almost begged you, to marry me."

"You asked me . . . *what?*"

"To marry me. I came close, stood behind you . . . . but you were deaf to me that night."

"Right," he said. "I was deaf. Concussion. I'd been knocked over in the blitz, the day after we quarreled. Not hurt, but I was deaf for months. I didn't know you came back to the garden! No wonder you hated me—even enough to marry Jeff. But the same thing that you took away from me, gave you back. I could read your lips tonight. I learned that trick in my deafness, I heard you say, 'Send him back to me.' I heard you say you loved me. And I was so happy—so glad. I believed again in the goodness of women and in the great kindness of God."

She came again, slowly, close into his arms and rested her head on his shoulder. His hand stroked the thick braids of her hair. The fire flickered low, the wind's keening had a softer tone and now they could hear the music the stars make on this night.

•

Louis Arthur Cunningham (1900–1954) of Saint John, New Brunswick, was one of the most popular and prolific Canadian authors of his time, writing more than 30 novels and 500 short stories.

A STOLEN CHRISTMAS

CHARLES M. SHELDON

Christmas for the Gray family no longer held any surprises: everyone knew ahead of time what each would receive. And each year, the amount of money paid for those gifts continued to escalate. Affluence had taken all the joy out of Christmas.

This year was just as bad or worse—until the unexpected happened.

Careful now, John," said Mrs. Mary Gray as her big, tall husband stood on tiptoe and leaned over to fasten a small object on the very top of the Christmas tree.

The object was a gilt paper angel blowing a silver trumpet on which were the words, "Glory to God in the highest!"

John fastened it securely, after several trials. After descending the ladder, and stepping back, he gave a deep sigh, and said, "How do you like it, Mary?"

"Lovely! Beautiful! Splendid!" said Mary, using up three of her best adjectives at once.

"Well, I hope it will do," replied John soberly.

"Of course it will do. What makes you talk so!" said Mary with a tone of reproach.

"Well, you know it is so different from what it used to be. There are no happy surprises for the children any more. Rob has been teasing for that gun for two months, and he knows he is going to get it. And Dorothy picked out that speaking doll two weeks ago, and she knows what it is. And Paul opened the package containing his automobile when it came up the other day. There's not much fun getting Christmas presents any more. It's an old story by the time you have them."

"You old growler," said Mary. "You are tired. Let's go into the library and rest. The tree itself will be a surprise, won't it? The children don't know about *that*."

"I hope not," replied John as they went out and shut the door.

They passed through the sitting-room into the library and sat down on opposite sides of a reading table, and Mrs. Gray looked a little anxiously at her husband.

"You don't begrudge the work of giving the children a happy time at Christmas, do you, John?"

"Of course not. You wouldn't think so if you saw me getting that tree. I wanted one thing that I got myself, instead of buying it, and you know what a job I had getting it from Fisher's Cove. I believe the children will be surprised when they see it. But it doesn't seem quite natural to light it up in the morning."

"We must, though. We promised them their presents in the morning. You're sure you didn't forget anything?"

"Pretty sure," replied John gravely. "Want me to go over the list? High-class repeating rifle for Rob. Automatic speaking, singing and walking doll for Dorothy. Real gasoline toy engine automobile for Paul. Two pounds of assorted candy for each. Then there is the warship, exact copy of the *Kansas*, with real guns and powder, for Rob and Paul together. Football and head-gear for Rob. Reflectoscope for Paul. Card-case for Dorothy, and two bottles of perfumery. *The Bandit of the Sierras* for Paul. Complete china tea-set for Dorothy, with electric lamps for the table. Besides what you hung up for me and what I hung up for you."

"John," said Mary coaxingly, "what was that queer-looking bundle you hung on the big limb near the window? Was that for me?"

"You're as bad as the children," said John laughing. "What do you want to know for?"

"I can't wait till morning, John; *tell* me."

"No, ma'am. I won't do it. Can't you wait a few hours? It's almost eleven now. The children will be awake in six hours and we will all come down together. That's the plan, isn't it?"

"Yes. Oh, well, I can wait. It's something pretty, I hope."

"I hope it is," said John anxiously.

"Because, John, you remember last Christmas you got me that patented dishwasher that broke everything into bits when you turned the handle."

"That was because I read the directions wrong and turned the thing backwards," said John hastily.

"Well, I hope you have got me something lovely this time. I have yours."

"What is it, Mary? *Tell* me."

"You're as bad as I am. No, sir. You'll have to wait. There's one thing I feel sorry about, though; I wish you hadn't got that gun for Rob. I'm in mortal terror he will shoot himself or somebody else."

"Of course not. If he is going to be an American citizen he has got to learn how to handle firearms. He may be a brigadier-general or an admiral someday."

"I hope not, John. Besides, I have been wondering a little lately if guns and warships are appropriate Christmas presents."

"Oh, pshaw, Mary! Anything is appropriate if you have the money to get it. The main thing about Christmas time is getting something. The bother is to know what to get. The gun won't hurt Rob any more than the candy."

"You got too much of that. Just think, John, two pounds apiece. And Uncle Terry always sends in such a lot of candy every Christmas."

"Oh, well, we can give some of it to Lizzie. She never has enough. Or else send it out to the poor-farm."

"Yes, that's what we will do," declared Mary.

"Well," said John as he rose, yawning, "let's have one more look at the tree before we go up."

He and his wife went to the door and opened it. John turned on the electric lights and he and Mary stepped into the room.

At first they could not grasp the obvious fact. John rubbed his eyes and opened them again. Mary ran forward with a sudden cry, and then stood in the middle of the room.

The Christmas tree was *gone*, and everything that had been hung on it and placed at its foot! Not a thing was left except a few broken strings of popcorn, two or three wax candles, a shred or two of gaudy tinsel and bits of evergreen. The tree itself was simply gone, and Mary ran forward to the big window that opened on the side veranda. It stood wide open, and other fragments of the tree and its trimmings were littered on the broad window sill. In the middle of the sill, resting calmly on its side, was the gilt paper angel and its trumpet, the only thing left behind intact.

"John, oh, John, someone has stolen our tree!" cried Mary as the full enormity of the event became clear. She ran to the open window but John was there before her. He leaped out upon the veranda. Bits of evergreen and small strings of popcorn showed which way the thief or thieves had gone, straight across the lawn, out to the middle of the road, and there the trail ceased.

"They had a wagon!" gasped John.

Mary had followed to the edge of the curb. "Quick, John! Run in and telephone the police station. They may catch them yet. Oh, to think of our Christmas—"

John was already in the house snatching at the receiver.

Did you ever have to telephone to a fire station that your house was afire and you wanted the department to hurry up before the house was burned to the ground? Then you can sympathize with John Gray on this Christmas Eve as he waited what seemed to him like a whole hour before he heard a lazy voice say, "Yes, this is the police station."

"Say! Send a man or two right out here quick. Someone has stolen our Christmas."

"What!"

"Send someone right out here quick. Our Christmas has been robbed, stolen, do you hear?"

"Yes. Stolen! What has been stolen?"

"Christmas!"

"Christmas what!"

"Oh, John!" broke in Mary, wringing her hands and crying hysterically. "Tell the man it is our tree, our tree, our Christmas tree that's gone."

"Tree!" roared John. "Christmas tree. Someone has stolen our Christmas tree. Do you get that?"

"Free?" came over the wire.

"No. Tree! Tree! Christmas tree! Send someone right out here, will you?"

"Out where?"

"Out here!"

"Where is it?"

"Oh, give him the name and number, John!" Mary cried again.

"John Gray. 719 Plymouth Avenue. Come quick, won't you?"

"All right. Be out there with the patrol."

John hung up the receiver and turned to Mary. She had sunk into a chair and was sobbing. At the sight, John began to recover some of his wits.

"Don't cry, Mary. The police will get them. They can't have had much of a start."

"But who would steal a Christmas tree? It might be some prank of the Raymond boys."

"No, I don't believe they would do that. Besides, you know Raymond never lets them stay out after nine o'clock, and here it is nearly midnight."

"What shall we *do*? How can we keep Christmas? To think of all those presents—" Mary broke down again at the thought.

"I hope the six-shooter and the warship will go off together and kill 'em," muttered John vindictively.

"And there was your present to me," said Mary with a groan. Now I shall never get it."

"Maybe you will. I can get another."

"Oh, why couldn't you go down town and buy some more things?" cried Mary suddenly.

"Too late," John replied gloomily. "Besides, the stores are all closing up. And besides, I haven't the money to buy any more six-shooters and real toy automobiles."

"But what will the children do?" asked Mary desperately. "Here we are without a single thing for them. It will break their hearts to have a Christmas and no presents."

"Maybe we could borrow a few of the Morgans'. They always have stacks more than they need."

Mary was about to reply indignantly to this levity on John's part when the patrol car arrived. Two officers came in, and John and Mary answered questions and showed them the place where the tree had stood, and where they were sitting when it was stolen, and where all traces of it had ceased in the road.

After the officers had examined all the evidence and had departed, after solemn promises to do all in their power to catch the thieves, John and Mary heard the clock strike the half hour.

"We shall never see that tree again," declared Mary resignedly. "Now what shall we do? We must have *something* for the children. I am going to make some candy."

"It's half past midnight," objected John.

"I don't care. I can make some from mother's recipe, in the chafing-dish."

Mary went out into the kitchen, and John, after standing irresolute a minute, went upstairs. He peeped into the boys' bedroom as he turned on the hall light. They were sleeping peacefully, and on Rob's placid face there was anything but the warlike look of a brigadier-general or an admiral.

Mr. Gray turned out the light and went on up another flight of stairs to his den. He sat down at an old desk, pulled out various drawers, and took out half a dozen articles, wrapping each one carefully and marking them with the children's names. He gathered them up and came downstairs.

Mary was busy over the chafing-dish.

"I've thought of a plan," said John, spreading out the articles on the table. "You put the candy in their stockings and one of these in each. Then we'll hide the rest somewhere and ask them to find them after dinner. There's that Chinese god Colfax sent me last year from Tientsin, and the little box of Japanese water flowers that has never been opened, and the fairy-tales Graves sent us from Tokyo. I've been keeping them for rainy days, and the children have never seen them."

"Just the thing!" exclaimed Mary with enthusiasm. "Oh, John, you are the brightest man—except when at the telephone. I never knew you to get a message straight, yet. But what shall we tell the children about the tree?"

"Tell them the truth," said John wisely. "The excitement will keep them from thinking about their loss."

That was the strangest Christmas the Gray family had ever spent. Before five o'clock three children were sitting up wide awake. Rob whispered to his brother. "I know what they've got. A tree. Father tried to sneak it into the barn two nights ago, but I saw him. Let's go down and turn on the light before Father and Mother wake up. I want to see my gun."

"And I want to start my automobile," said Paul, hastily climbing out of bed.

"And I want to wind up my doll and hear it cry," said Dorothy.

The three white figures stole downstairs with no more noise than that made by Rob as he fell over a rug in the hall.

They opened the door in the parlor and turned on the light and stared. Instead of a beautiful tree they saw the well-known furniture of the room and nothing else, except three stockings hanging from the parlor mantel.

Their astonished exclamations awakened their parents. When they came down, the matter was explained. The boys looked very sober. But as the family sat down to breakfast, Dorothy relieved the seriousness by leaving her place, going over to her father and saying, "What if those wicked men had shot you and Mother. That would have been even worse, wouldn't it?"

"I believe it would, for *us*," said John Gray with a laugh which changed into a half-sob when Dorothy put her arms around his neck and kissed him.

They were all at breakfast when their nearest neighbor, Mark Raymond, came in.

"Just read about your loss in the paper! It's the meanest thing I ever heard of. But I've found one of the things. I was out early and saw this bundle lying close in by the curb in front of my house, and it has your name written on it, Mrs. Gray."

"Oh, my present!" exclaimed Mary. It was the queer-shaped package she had asked John about. She hastily cut the string and unwrapped the package.

"What is it?" she said when it was uncovered.

"It's a combination towel rack and shaving mirror and—"

But that was about as far as John got. Everybody roared, Mark Raymond with the rest. Rob got hold of the combination and tried to work it, and something caught his fingers and pinched them. They all roared again—except Rob. Mary laughed until she cried. When they could not laugh any more, Mark Raymond rose to go.

"Well, no use to wish you folks a Merry Christmas. You seem to be having one all right."

"We've got one another," said Mary, looking mischievously at John. "I don't believe any other man in town would buy his wife a towel rack and shaving mirror combined."

John looked a little disturbed at first, then his face cleared up. "You see, Raymond, my wife is different from all the rest. She can take a joke even when it isn't meant."

Raymond looked at Gray with hesitation. Then he spoke suddenly. "Say, Gray, can you—would you and Mrs. Gray go to church this morning, if you had an invitation?"

"Church!"

"Yes. You see I belong to the Brotherhood at church. You know Reverend Strong. Well, he is holding a Christmas morning service. Lots of good music and a short sermon. Mr. Vinge plays the organ. The English have Christmas Day services in their churches and everybody goes."

John Gray looked undecided. "Oh, I don't know. I'm not much of a church-goer, as you know, Raymond."

"That's the reason I'm asking you," said Raymond with a smile. "Be delighted to have you come. Both of you."

"Why not?" said Mrs. Gray. "Lizzie will get dinner. No one has stolen our turkey. I saw it go into the oven. And I like to hear Strong."

Rob spoke eagerly. "Did you say Mr. Vinge is going to play the organ?"

"Yes," said Raymond.

"I want to hear him," said Rob, who was music-loving in spite of his warlike proclivities. "Can't I go?"

"Me, too," chimed in Paul.

"I won't stay here alone. I want to go too," said Dorothy.

"We'll all go," said Mary decidedly.

"I don't care," laughed John, "it's a queer Christmas to start with and might as well be queer to go on with. I never went to church on Christmas in my life."

"Won't hurt you," said Raymond much pleased. "Sit with my folks. We are all going."

So, an hour later, John Gray and his wife and their children were in church with their neighbors, the Raymonds.

John Gray felt a little bewildered. But he had been more or less bewildered ever since he opened the parlor door to find the Christmas tree stolen. As the service went on, the beauty of it crept in upon him. The church was trimmed with wreaths, and up near the pulpit was a tree, shapely and benignant, with no presents on it, but lighted with small electric lamps and tinged with white. Vinge, the blind organist, sat at his beloved instrument. What melody flowed out of it! The Christmas glory flooded his keys.

John glanced at his wife. Her face was wrapped with tender feeling. "Glory to God in the Highest," sang the children's choir. The fresh young voices were fragrant of Bethlehem and the Nativity. Gray looked along at his children. Rob, the warlike, was lost to all the world, his boyish face upturned to catch all sound, his eyes fixed on Vinge, his soul caught in the meshes of that blind man's harmony. Something choked John Gray. What if some time his boy should be a great organ player! What fine children God had given him!

His glance came back to his wife. What a lovely face she had. What a beautiful mother she had always been. How devoted to her husband. How proud of him in spite of his awkward blunders and his many faults. He quietly reached for her hand, and thrilled at the clasp of her warm, firm fingers. She smiled at him and then together they listened to Phillips Brooks' most beautiful hymn: "O little town of Bethlehem, How still we see thee lie," and again a little later in the service they joined their voices with the congregation, as they sang,

"Angels from the realms of glory
Wing your flight o'er all the earth."

Then the sermon touched them. Even the children could understand it, it was so simple, and so clear in telling what Christ meant to the earth.

When the service closed in a quiet moment of worship, the people rose silently and went out. At the door Gray exchanged greetings with several friends, and as he walked along home, said to his wife, "Say, Mary, I liked that. Wonder why the churches in America don't have Christmas Day services more generally."

"It meant more to me than I can tell, John. Somehow I feel younger and happier. Doesn't that seem queer, when all our presents were stolen except mine?"

They both laughed.

"We have each other," said John gently.

"And the children," said Mary.

"And the children," said John.

After dinner, the children hunted for the other articles their father had hidden. They were simple things, saved for rainy-day use, but they were real surprises. Near the big window in search of her present, Dorothy discovered the gilt angel with the trumpet. It had lain peacefully there during all the excitement.

Mrs. Gray put it on the mantel over the clock. Later in the day, while the children were out in the kitchen cracking some nuts Rob had stored in the barn last fall, she said to John, "I believe that angel has something to do with our happiness. Doesn't it seem strange to you, John? It was a dreadful loss, but we don't seem to be feeling so dreadful about it. After all, the boys never got the gun or the warship. And they don't seem to feel so very bad."

A shout of laughter came from the kitchen where some of the Raymond children were visiting with the Grays and showing them their presents. And they could hear Dorothy say in a tone of superiority, "But that's nothing. We had a burglar in our house last night!"

"It does seem strange," said John. "The police just phoned that they can get no clue to the robbery. It's been a very different sort of Christmas. Mary, what were you going to give me in exchange for the towel rack?"

"Go up to your den and find it," said Mary shyly.

John went up, two steps at a time. On his writing-desk he found it. A photograph of his wife framed in an old-gold oval frame which had belonged to her mother.

When he came down he was met by Mary at the foot of the stairs.

"Oh, John, do you like it? And it's a surprise to me, too. I thought it was gone with the rest. But when you went through the window I saw my present to you on the veranda, and saved it for a surprise. Do you know another woman in town who wouldn't have told?"

"No, I don't. And I don't know another like you in any way." And John kissed his wife, who actually blushed for happiness.

Later in the evening, as the family sat in front of the fire eating nuts and apples, Mrs. Gray asked Dorothy to go into the library and bring a box she would find on the big table.

When it was brought in, Mrs. Gray asked Dorothy to open it. Faded tissue-paper wrappings came off. And there lay an old-fashioned doll dressed in India muslin, with quaint ribbons under a Converse hat. Dorothy was overcome. Mary whispered to John, "Bessie's doll. I haven't had the heart to give it to anyone until today."

A tear fell on John's hand as the memory of their first child crept into the firelight and softened the glow of that new Christmas. Later, when the children were asleep, Dorothy hugging the India muslin doll up to her cheek, John said to Mary as they came down and sat by the fire again: "After all, we have had a beautiful day, Mary. We have one another."

"And the children," said Mary.

And the firelight flung a flame a little higher than the rest so that the trumpet of the gilt angel stood out very clear with the words, "Glory to God in the highest and on earth peace among men in whom he is well pleased."

Then there stole into the hearts of John Gray and Mary Gray, his wife, at the close of that blessed Christmas Day something more like the Peace of God than they had ever known. The Child Christ meant more to them than He had ever meant. And in their hearts they both yearned for a better life, glorified by Him who is the peace of those whose hearts are restless, and the joy of those whose hearts are sad.

•

Charles M. Sheldon (1857–1946), clergyman and author. Besides being editor of *The Christian Herald*, he wrote a number of books, including one of the mega bestsellers of his time, *In His Steps.*

Christmas Memories

GUEST IN THE HOUSE

HELEN MARIE AMENRUD

Edie was determined: since Joe had invited the Widdams for Christmas Eve, and since she wanted to impress these sophisticated new neighbors of theirs, she'd break with family traditions and replace them with more modern ones.

But Joe put his foot down. No! The old ways must remain.

So Edie prepared for disaster.

Joe's reaction to the pink Christmas tree was a flat and stubborn, "No!" And she had been doing it all for him, too, just so they could make a nice impression on the Widdams, but that Joe was such a stick-in-the-mud.

Edie had started to plan the special Christmas Eve the night Joe first told her he wanted Clarice and Ed Widdam for Christmas. Even while she was protesting that the house was too small and too plain to entertain their sophisticated new neighbors, she was working on her list.

She *had* to make a good impression. The Widdams were obviously people who did things the right way. Their new rambler house was the ramblingest in the neighborhood; their attached garage held two shining cars. Just meeting smartly dressed Clarice Widdam in the super market made Edie feel all helter-skelter and almost dowdy. And Joe wanted the Widdams for Christmas Eve.

"They were tickled, honey," Joe told Edie when she reminded him again that their own Collins family Christmas was so old-fashioned. "This is their first Christmas here since Ed was transferred, and they haven't been here long enough to really know anybody. And Ed loves kids, Edie! He even wants to help out coaching one of the kid baseball teams this summer."

"Oh, goody," Edie said bitingly, "that's how we'll entertain them then. We'll have a ball game. With Uncle Maynard and Aunt Helen and Cousin Fred, we'll have just enough for a team!" Edie was furious with Joe. Any other time she would have been delighted—but Christmas!

There would be Uncle Maynard and Aunt Helen, each with the latest in aches and pains and their respective remedies. Joe's cousin, Fred, a most uninteresting but kindly soul, would come with his drugstore-wrapped parcels and his wordy explanations of why the large-sized colognes were really the practical buy. The children would be wound up like tops and every good manner and really natural charm would be lost in the mix-up.

Everything for Edie started with a list, so she wrote down every detail of a simple but charmingly served dinner. She planned the children's time so they would not get out of hand. She had revised, rewritten, re-planned, and reorganized until the list was perfect. And now she couldn't find it!

"Where did I put it?" she asked herself desperately as she ransacked all the known tuck-away places in the house. Maybe the children would know. They certainly could find anything else that was hidden away.

"Connie!" Edie really didn't expect an answer, because 11-year-old Connie had a deafness that could be turned on and off according to the tone of her mother's voice. Today she responded promptly and she trailed in dragging four feet of shower curtain behind her.

"Connie, what in the world are you supposed to be?" Again expecting no answer, Edie went on, "Have you seen my list?"

"Which one?" Connie asked absently as she posed before the wall mirror. "What list are you talking about?"

"The list of things to do for Christmas. I can't find anything in this clutter."

The living room did have that Friday-afternoon look, plus a little extra disorder of the rewrapped gift parcels brought home from school parties. This was the Friday before Christmas, but more important to Edie, it was the Friday before Widdams!

"I see Bill has been home, too," Edie muttered, glancing at a pair of ice skates, a wad of damp towels and something that looked like a rusty trap lying just inside the living room door. "To him, home is just one big closet."

"Billy's walking a girl home," giggled Connie, now completely swathed in shower curtain.

"That's nice," Edie drawled. "I hope she inspires him to comb his hair and tuck in his shirt tail."

"She's drippy, and so is Bill." Now Connie had one of Edie's brass candlesticks aloft in one hand.

"O.K., Connie, I give up! What are you, the Statue of Liberty?"

"Mother! Don't you know a Wise Man when you see one?" Connie was shocked with her mother's lack of appreciation.

"Nope, I guess not! I don't get to meet many wise men—not lately, anyway."

"This is a *Bible* Wise Man! It's for the church play! You forgot!"

Oh, dear, I almost did, Edie thought, but she said, "Not really, dear. Do you know your part?"

"Mine and everyone else's, too," retorted Connie in the know-it-all tone that Edie found unbearable at times. "Is this how a Wise Man should look, Mom?"

"Exactly, dear, and now please BE one and remember where you saw the list."

"I saw it in your hand, that's where, and I think it's silly. A list for what we do at Christmas! We always do the same things!" Now she was Connie again, and the shower curtain was just a shower curtain.

That's just the trouble, thought Edie, *we always do the same things.* But this year had to be different. She'd *have* to make a new list, that's all.

The sound of the piano in the playroom started. "Oh, no," she groaned, "not that again!"

Two months ago, 8-year-old Carol had balked like a young mule at every reminder to practice her piano lessons. Suddenly, it was different. She had burst into the house two weeks ago, brown eyes shining, crying, "I have a special piece! For two hands! With runs 'n' everything!"

To Edie, Carol's lessons proved no musical ability, merely showed her to be ambidextrous, with her left and right hands working completely independent of each other. Sometimes Edie was sure they were playing two different pieces. But Carol plugged along, counting her one-and-ah, two-and-ah's almost as loudly as she played those unmatched notes. Today it was just too much.

"Carol! Carol, please!" Edie had to wait for the two-and-ah before she could be heard. Surprisingly, Carol's square little figure appeared promptly.

"Hi, Mom. Where you been? We had a party at school, and we each got a autograph book from Miss Buckley, and we brought home our decorations for our own tree!"

And there they were, wrapped in her sturdy little arms—yards and yards of orange-red paper links! *Oh, no,* thought Edie, *not ORANGE!*

"They're very pretty, honey," Edie said evenly, "but wouldn't you like to have them in the playroom instead?"

"Oh, no, Mom! They're for everyone, not just me! Connie has so many more things on the tree than I do."

Carol's voice told how much the crudely made chain meant to her, and Edie could picture the dark, shining head bent over the task of making this "for everyone."

"Of course, honey. We'll keep it with all the other Christmas things." Edie resolved to find some place for the chain, Widdams or no Widdams.

The big box taken from the storage closet each year held a wealth of these treasures, each marked carefully, "Billy, first grade," or "Connie, kindergarten," and so on. Each Christmas found the keepsakes a little more worn and defaced but a little more precious.

The box presented a real problem for Edie this year, because the first item on her list had been the pink Christmas tree. That's when Joe shot sparks.

"Whoever heard of a pink Christmas tree!" His nice, Irish-y face was anything but nice right then. "Listen, Edie, the Widdams are coming here to spend OUR Christmas in OUR way. That does not include a pink Christmas tree!"

"Oh, Joe, just once can't we do something with a little flair to it?" Edie begged. Joe was unmovable.

"Honey, you can flair all over the place, but you know the kids have had their eyes on a tree in Carlson's woods for a long time. The tree-chopping trip is a part of Christmas, and the kids love it. And so do I. No pink Christmas tree!"

"All right, then. Be stubborn. You know I'm planning everything just for the Widdams." Her voice was at the near-tear stage, and her cheeks were flushed.

"Well, my pet, you can UNplan everything then. It's Christmas the old way." And Joe's voice said that ended that.

So it was going to be the regular, ordinary green Christmas tree with Connie's kindergarten angel and Bill's lopsided stars made from tin-can covers and Carol's orange-red chain and all the other off-colored contributions with their dabs of paste and fingerprints still showing.

It isn't that we'd never use them again, Edie's conscience whispered. *It's just that this year was to be so special!*

Joe shot more sparks over the menu. "What do you mean, roast beef?" he asked as he read the list over her shoulder. "What's the matter with *Lutfisk*?"

"But, Joe, you never liked *Lutfisk* when we were first married," Edie protested. "And the smell!"

"Well, I like it now—smell and all!" Joe's voice softened as he went on. "As far as not liking it, honey, it was just that it was new to me. I never had any Christmas traditions until you showed me. Christmas dinner off a menu, that's what I had. And now *Lutfisk* is part of our Christmas."

Edie felt a little ashamed because she remembered too that Joe, who had lived in a succession of rooming houses with his widowed father, had never known the warmth of a family Christmas until their marriage. She had loved his delight and surprise as each new tradition had been introduced, and she had felt a little proud that she could bring a real Christmas feeling into his life.

So, the list had been changed: GREEN CHRISTMAS TREE. LUTFISK.

A banging in the hall interrupted her thoughts. Bill's half-bass, half-treble voice called out, "We're home!"

"You're telling me," she muttered, but she called, "Welcome! You can start in by putting away your share of the loot stowed around here!"

"You sound crabby, Mom," Bill said, as he added a cap and jacket to the mound on the floor.

"I'm in a boy-eating mood, my lad, so do as you're told. You, too," she added as she helped 5-year-old Rog with his snowsuit.

Oh dear, she thought as they went up the stairs. *Don't let me get owly over this.*

Friday night was meeting night for everyone but Edie and Rog, so after his bath and story and prayers and three drinks of water, plus a last minute summons to ask if "Santa Claus had any REAL children of his own," Edie was alone. By the time Joe and the children came home, the new list was ready, and there wasn't a thing on it to get excited about. *It'll be the same old Christmas to us, but the* Lutfisk *and the decorations will probably make it the most unusual one the Widdams ever spent,* Edie thought grimly, as she tumbled into bed beside the sleeping Joe.

Early Saturday morning, Joe and the children went after the tree. Back in two hours, singing noisily, they tramped through the house like a parade. Then the whole family had a hand in decorating. Though Edie pitched in reluctantly, she soon was giggling with the rest over the yield of the treasure box.

"Pretty crummy looking stable," Bill muttered, but his face shone at the family's staunch denials.

Just let that Clarice Widdam look down her nose at it! Edie thought. Bill placed the crudely carved lamb and burro in front of the stable he had made from wooden cheese boxes.

"Here's my angel! Where does it go?" squealed Connie.

"Same place as always, Hon," Joe told her. "Right on top." And he reached up to place the faded and wilting angel in the uppermost branch.

Next came Bill's stars and Carol's orange-red chain, and then round-eyed Rog cried, "My twinklers!" and Edie helped him to reach up with his paper spirals that bounced like springs and really did twinkle with bits of sequins.

One by one, the treasures were discovered anew. The *Tomte Gabbe*—and Edie was touched to hear Joe tell Rog that this was NOT Santa Claus, but a little elf that Edie's mother, Grandma Hanson, had brought from Sweden. The *Jul Bok*, raggedy now and brittle, but again Edie had to tell the story of how in Sweden every home has a large straw goat in the yard during the holiday season. A space was cleared on the mantle for the *Angla Spel*, and after the brass was polished, Connie set the four little candles in place, and Joe touched a match to each wick. The *Angla Spel* was a favorite with the children, and they loved to watch as the heat of the candle flames started the four chubby angels spinning round and round, each with a wand that touched a little brass chime. "Now it SOUNDS like Christmas, too," Carol breathed ecstatically.

Then Joe snapped the switch for the lights. "Oh," breathed the children in unison, as the soft blues and reds and golds of the tiny lamps were reflected in the shimmering tinsel. "It's the most beautiful tree ever!" *It is pretty,* Edie thought, *but I did want a pink one with silver ornaments!*

Sunday brought Aunt Helen, complete with cold tablets and liniment and worn out from her bus trip from Duluth. Once Uncle Maynard appeared, though, she fell into a lively swap of symptoms that brought a healthy glow to her eyes. She was not to be outdone, whatever ailment he named, she had one more serious!

At least I don't have to worry about entertaining them, thought Edie. *But the Widdams will get one look at us and one whiff of that* Lutfisk *plus Aunt Helen's liniment, and they'll think we came over on the last boat!*

Cousin Fred, always a favorite with the children, arrived with his pockets bulging and his red face wreathed in smiles, and quickly escaped to the playroom where the racket became almost unbearable. Even Joe, who had stoutly defended Carol's musical ability, finally begged her to stop. "You'd think she could play something besides that tune," he complained cheerfully, as a loud "one-and-ah" was accompanied by a halting run.

Rog darted in and out on mysterious errands. A *rope*. A *knife*. Connie wanted to borrow Edie's coral beads. Bill *needed* a flashlight. And so the day went, and suddenly it was Monday and the day of Christmas Eve. The day of the Widdams.

"This one day should have twenty-four hours all between lunch and dinner," Edie said as she rushed through the house. She scarcely had the last bit of holly tacked in place when the Widdams arrived.

Ed Widdam was hearty and friendly, and the children took him over at once. Clarice Widdam smiled sweetly and thanked Edie for allowing them to come. "I told Ed it was almost too much to expect," she said in her soft voice, "but I think the idea of having children around at Christmas was a temptation that overcame his good manners."

"Oh, but we *wanted* you," Edie replied eagerly, and she found herself meaning it.

Clarice was generous in her compliments about the house and the children, and she won Aunt Helen completely with her sympathy. *She's a lady, all right,* Edie thought.

Everything went well, and Joe beamed with pride as the children pointed out the treasures on the tree. "The twinklers are mine," Rog told them proudly, "but they're for everyone."

"And I made the chain," Carol added, "and Connie made the angel when she was only six years old."

"Such a Christmas-y angel, too," Clarice Widdam said.

"I'll have to make a new manger next year," Bill said in his half-man voice, and making an awkward attempt to explain the crude stable.

"But you must always keep this one, Bill," Clarice told him. "It's the very first one you made; that makes it special." Edie thanked her silently with her eyes.

The room looked like Christmas. The little *Angla Spel* tinkled away merrily and the festive glow of the tree shone on the happy faces in the room.

Suddenly Clarice Widdam exclaimed, "What IS that I smell?"

Edie's heart went plop! *I knew it,* she thought. *Here goes our nice impression!*

"It's *Lutfisk,*" Joe said. And he made it sound like pheasant under glass. "We have it every year. It's Scandinavian, you know,"

"Indeed I do know," answered Clarice, "and it's years since I've had it." At Edie's look of surprise, Clarice continued, "I'm one of those Minnesota Swedes you hear about, and I used to see the *Lutfisk* stacked like cord wood outside my father's grocery store. The weather would be cold enough to keep it until it was taken home and soaked for hours. Then it was trimmed and tied in a cheesecloth bag and cooked in a huge kettle and soon we'd smell it all over the house. That wonderful, wonderful smell!"

Edie felt weak. *And I was for beef,* she thought. "I'm so glad you like it. For us, it wouldn't be Christmas without *Lutfisk*—even my big Irishman loves it." And from her big Irishman she received a wry and slightly accusing grin that made her squirm.

"And who wouldn't like it?" asked Clarice, daring anyone to speak up.

Aunt Helen, rejuvenated by the thought of food, added, "And it's so healthy. So easy to digest." Uncle Maynard just nodded and Cousin Fred beamed and said the way he liked *Lutfisk* was in large quantities.

And so dinner was a wonderful success. The chatter was gay and familyish, and the Widdams obviously enjoyed everything and everybody. As they left the table, Clarice Widdam said, "This is a Christmas I shall never forget. It is almost as though it were planned just for me."

It was, thought Edie, avoiding Joe's look—*for you, in spite of me and my big ideas.*

"It's time for the program!" sang out Rog, as the family and guests settled themselves in the living room.

Every Christmas Eve, right after dinner, and before any gifts were opened, the family sang carols and the children performed their parts from the church and school programs. Edie had hoped to postpone this little ceremony until after the guests' departure, and now she murmured, almost apologetically, "They love this part of Christmas."

"Why, of course they do," Clarice's eyes were sparkling and she applauded softly, encouraging the children to begin.

After a few minutes of whispered conference in the hall, Bill entered with a wooden box that he placed carefully at one end of the room. His back was turned, but when he moved aside, they could see the shaded glow of light that came from inside the box.

"It's a cradle," whispered Clarice. "They've made a cradle for their program."

So that's why they wanted a flashlight, Edie thought.

Bill left quietly, and serious little Rog entered. In childish, measured tones he recited his Sunday-school "Welcome One and All" poem and bowed formally during the applause that followed. Still unsmiling, Rog announced. "In a minute, we'll have a play—soon's I put my costume on. I have TWO parts, because there aren't enough of us to be everything." He did smile then, but a sibilant whisper from the hall restored his dignity, and he went on. "The people in the play are Miss Constance Collins; she's the Wise Man. Mr. William Collins is the shepherd, and I am—and Mr. Roger Collins is—the angel." At that moment, he looked like one. "Miss Carol Collins is the accompa—she plays the piano." He started to leave, but hesitated long enough to say, "We all wrote the play, only Connie did the most."

There was a little flurry of excitement in the hall, and then Carol entered and seated herself with dignity at the piano. She played a halting arrangement of "Silent Night" as the others came in. Connie, resplendent in the shower curtain and with Edie's coral beads holding a silk scarf on her head, led the procession. Thought Edie, *it really doesn't look like a shower curtain now.* In her hands, Connie held a long white scroll, and on her face was a look of reverence.

Next came Bill in Joe's striped bathrobe tied with a stout rope around his slim waist. His head was hooded and he carried Carol's old toy lamb under his arm. Rog came last, swathed in white, with two huge paper wings pinned to his back. On his head was a band of tinsel. As he took his place behind the cradle, the glow from within gave an added radiance to his sweet face and made the tinsel band truly a halo.

Connie read the Christmas story from her scroll. The children stood quietly, moving only as the lovely story progressed. They looked at the sky at the Star everyone felt was really there. They expressed the awe of the shepherds and the Wise Men. They knelt in adoration before the Manger of the Babe.

And then the piano started again. Edie sat straight and stiff as she recognized the long-practiced melody and she groped for Joe's hand. Carol's fingers seemed so sure, and though her lips counted the one-and-ah, two-and-ah's, she did not miss a note.

Forgive me, Edie thought. *They knew all the time what was really important about Christmas and I almost forgot. To think they had to show me again! It isn't pink Christmas trees or something you can put on a list. It isn't glitter and impressions. It's all this—love and sweetness and sharing.* She felt the understanding pressure of Joe's hand on hers, and with her eyes filled with happy tears, she listened to the children sing.

Sweetly and simply, their voices rang out in the words. *"Happy Birthday to You. Happy Birthday to You. Happy Birthday, Dear Jesus, Happy Birthday to You."*

•

Helen Marie Amenrud wrote for popular and inspirational magazines during the second half of the twentieth century.

ERIC'S GIFT

DEBORAH SMOOT

Why was it, the teacher wondered with a groan, *that the children did well on all the Christmas carols—all but one?*

If only Eric would sing the right words!

"Come, they told me, dum-ditty-dum-dum. . . ." I stopped the chorus of four-year-olds midstream in the song and looked directly at Eric. "Eric, this song is called 'The Little Drummer Boy.'" I spoke sternly, "and the words are 'Come, they told me, Pa-rum-pum-pum-pum,' not 'dum-ditty-dum-dum.' And, Eric, you don't need to yell. We can hear you above everyone else. Just sing, Eric. You know, sing!"

"Eric, Eric, Eric," I muttered under my breath as I walked back to the music stand.

Eric had two speeds: on and off. I never saw off. I imagined "off" happened for Eric sometime between one and three a.m. This shiny-faced wisp of a boy had more energy than any child I had ever met. He simply could not hold still. He shifted; he twitched; he giggled; he yawned; and, when he sang, he yelled.

He smelled of soap and Brylcreem, and of clothes that had been hung out on the line to dry. Two yellow-striped T-shirts, faded and frayed at the neck, one pair of black Levi's, and a red-hooded sweatshirt constituted his entire school wardrobe. But his clothes were always clean and pressed. Mornings at our public pre-school always found Eric scrubbed and polished, and ready for action. He was obviously loved.

And, I must admit, there was much about Eric that was lovable. Through all his perpetual motion, he smiled. In fact, he never quit smiling. His face carried a non-stop, tooth-filled grin. And when Eric's grin caught you head on, it was impossible to stay mad at him.

Three times a week, on the front row of the pre-school chorus, Eric stood grinning and yelling; although in all fairness to him, he thought he was singing! It's just that Eric loved to sing, and he belted out those Christmas songs as though his life depended on it. He raised the roof, if not our spirits.

There were, however, a couple of problems with that. One, Eric was one of eight children bused from the other side of town. His enthusiasm alone made him the uncontested "star" of the chorus. Some of the mothers were upset that one of those "other" children was stealing the show. Two, Eric could never remember the words. Because his enthusiasm made him a natural leader, soon the whole chorus was singing, "Come, they told me, dum-ditty-dum-dum," and then pealing off into uncontrolled laughter.

I was trying to work on both problems. I sent the words of the song home with Eric to memorize. And some of the mothers were making stiff, white collars with big red bows so this chorus of middle-class children sprinkled with the 'rag-tag bunch" (as one mother called them) would look unified, even if they didn't sound it!

The final rehearsal went well until we got to "The Little Drummer Boy."

"Come they told me," was followed by hesitation, then silence. The piano went on with the melody, but the four-year-olds were so confused with hum and dum and pum that they simply froze. Except for Eric. "Dum-ditty-dum-dum," he finished the phrase.

"That's it!" I screamed and stopped the chorus. "We are not singing about the seven dwarfs! This is a Christmas song, a *special* song about a little boy just like you—except that he lived long ago when Baby Jesus was born. He was poor, but he wanted more than anything to visit the newborn baby in the manger. When he got there, he saw kings and wise men waiting to see Baby Jesus. They all had expensive gifts to give the Christ child. Things like gold and jewels, and perfume. Well, when the boy saw all those fancy people, with all their expensive gifts, he just about turned around and went home. I mean, he was just a kid with nothing to give. About the only thing he could do was play his drum.

"But then he looked around and realized that Baby Jesus, too, was poor, that He was born in a stable (that's like a barn where they kept the animals). So, when it was the boy's turn to see Jesus, he asked if he could play his drum for the baby, and Mary said yes. Well, everyone loved it, and the boy learned that the best gift you can give is the gift of yourself!"

I finished the story and, satisfied that the children understood it, went on: "When we sing the song, we are making the sound of the little boy's drum. It is a 'p' sound. Everybody say it with me, 'pa, pa, pum.' Now everyone say, 'pum' twenty times."

While the chorus repeated the words, I looked at the clock. I had taken too long telling the story of the little drummer boy. Our rehearsal time was gone.

"Okay, children," I finished up, "there is no more time to practice, but you have to remember the drum makes a 'p' sound. They ran off to lunch, 'pumming' all the way.

I walked back to their classroom teacher, who was sitting on a chair at the rear of the auditorium, watching the rehearsal. Discouraged, I sat down beside her. "Tell me about Eric," I requested.

"Well, there isn't much to tell," she said. "As far as we know, he is an only child being raised by his grandmother. We've never met her. Eric told us she didn't want to come to 'Back to School Night' because she was afraid someone would find out she can't read. Apparently, his grandmother is an illiterate woman who stands in the shadows and, as best she can on a welfare check, loves and cares for her little boy." The teacher stood up. "I'd better check on the children," she finished. "Good luck, Debbi."

I went to the office to look up Eric's records. He lived alone wit his paternal grandmother. There was an address, but no phone number. I wrote a special note inviting her to the program and sent it home with Eric—pinned to his shirt so she would be sure to see it. Surely, if his grandmother couldn't read the note, she knew someone who could read it to her.

The day of the Christmas program arrived. The parents came armed with cameras and video recorders. I stood in the hall with the pre-school chorus. Eric had on a new white dress shirt that he wanted to show me. He was higher than a kite. The whole chorus was excited, wiggling even more than usual. The stiff white collars were driving them crazy. I barked out some last-minute instructions: "You are not to touch those collars while you are singing, even if you are itching to death!" That said, we all marched onto the stage.

Without a hitch, the children went through the songs: "Jingle Bells," "Silent Night," "Away in a Manger." This little crew looked and sounded, for all the world, like a chorus of angels. It's amazing what white collars and a touch of the Christmas spirit can do.

I turned the music on the stand to "The Little Drummer Boy," signaled the pianist to begin, and made the 'pum' sound with my lips to the children as the introduction was playing.

"Come, they told me . . ." they started right on cue. "Pum-ditty-pum-pum. . . ." They hesitated for a moment before joining Eric. There was no stopping them now. "I am a poor boy, too" . . . Eric's voice soared above the others, 'pum-ditty-pum-pum." *How could he have forgotten the Pa-rum-pum-pum part when I talked to them yesterday?* I could hear the audience snickering. "Mary nodded . . . pum-ditty-pum-pum. . . ." By now, only about three children were singing with Eric. The noise from the audience had scared the others. *What was I thinking? This song is way too hard for a group of four-year-olds.*

The children were frozen, and embarrassed, and so was I. We all wanted to crawl off stage, all except for Eric. "The ox and lamb kept time," he yelled, "pum-ditty-pum-pum." And he grinned and continued. "I played my drum for Him, pum-ditty-pum-pum." By now, Eric was singing a solo, "I played my best for Him." He didn't even seem to notice that no one else was singing. "Pum-ditty-pum-pum-ditty-pum-pum. . . . "

Eric's "pum dittys" were bouncing all around the auditorium. The laughter in the audience was now uncontrollable. Finally, and I mean finally, the song ended, and a bunch of bewildered four-year-olds bowed and got off the stage as fast as possible, totally out of order.

Before I could get out of the school, the hallway filled with parents and children in white collars. Leading the pack was Eric, pulling a short gray-haired woman by the hand.

Eric made a beeline for me. "Mrs. Smoot, this is my grandma." He dragged her up to my side and grinned. "She rode the bus all the way here to see the program." He was obviously pleased that she had made the trip. "She wants to tell you thanks!" he yelled.

I turned to his grandmother and started to speak.

"Well, I'm happy to meet you," I said. "Eric is . . ." There was a vacant stare in her bright eyes. I noticed large hearing aids in both her ears. She smiled, obviously confused.

"She says she's happy to meet you, too," Eric blurted out. He was acting as a translator for his grandmother, who I now realized was almost totally deaf. "Boy, isn't Christmas great, Mrs. Smoot?" Eric continued. "Sorry I sang so loud, but that song about the little drummer boy is such a great story, I wanted my grandma to hear it!"

Eric's grandmother didn't seem to hear a word we were saying. But, standing there silently in a purple-flowered dress, she could see Eric's excitement and his love of the music. She looked at me for a moment, her eyes filled with tears, and spontaneously reached up to hug me. "Thank you," she whispered.

"Thank you," I said back as I looked in her eyes. "Thank you for Eric." I embraced her again.

Tenderly, she then removed Eric's white collar, handed it to me and took her grandson's hand. I watched them walk down the hall. Eric bouncing at her side and singing, "Pum-ditty-pum-pum" all the way out the door.

I never hear "The Little Drummer Boy" without remembering Eric's gift to his grandmother and her gift of unconditional love to him. I never read the story of that little drummer boy without recalling the miracle in the manger: God's greatest gift of all—His love. I realize that, when I sometimes tune Him out, God yells His love to me. And every time I sing this carol, though I don't sing it that way out loud, in my heart the words will always be "pum-ditty-pum-pum."

•

Deborah Smoot writes today from her home in Park City, Utah.

Christmas Memories

PANDORA'S BOOKS

JOSEPH LEININGER WHEELER

I'd always wanted to write a Christmas romance set in a used bookstore guarded by a cat. As always, I asked God for the plot—and thus was born "Pandora's Books."

PROLOGUE

Later it would be remembered as "the year with no spring." All the more surprising because it had been a bitterly cold winter, complete with record snow-fall, frequent ice-storms, traffic gridlock on the Washington, D.C., Beltway, closed airports, and snow days—longed-for by children and teachers alike.

At first, people assumed it to be a fluke: *surely* the geese couldn't possibly be flying north already! Why the iced-over Potomac and Severn Rivers were only now beginning to break up. But the honking geese kept coming, attuned to their planet's moods in ways humans will never understand.

Surely the cherry blossoms down on the Tidal Basin couldn't possibly be blooming this early! And the daffodils too? . . . But they were—and those who delayed but a day missed Jefferson's lagoon at its loveliest, for unseasonably warm air, coupled with sudden wind, stripped the blossoms from the unbelieving trees.

Azaleas and dogwood were next—way too early, as well. Usually, the multi-hued azalea, along with dogwood of pink and white, ravish the senses for weeks every spring—not so this year: they came and went in only days. By early April, the thermometer had already climbed to 100, and now schools began to close because of the heat instead of the cold.

Once entrenched, the heat dug in. And the mercury kept climbing. Even the spring rains failed to come; and farmers shook their heads, trembling in their mortgages. Plants dried up, lawns turned brown, in spite of frequent watering—and centuries-old trees dropped their already yellowish leaves in abject defeat.

Tourists stayed home, making sizzling Washington a veritable ghost town. For the first time in recent memory, one could park anywhere one went—no waiting, no endless circling.

And for those Washingtonians who did not have air-conditioning in home, office, and cars, it was hell. One couldn't even escape by boat, for prolonged calms plagued the Chesapeake, interspersed by blasting gales of fierce, tinder-dry winds.

On TV weather maps, the entire eastern seaboard turned brown in early April—and stayed brown, altering only to a deeper hue of brown. There was a morbid fascination in watching as heat record after heat record fell before that immovable front, seemingly set in concrete.

So . . . when the weather reporters trumpeted the glad news that, come Memorial Day weekend, the siege would at last be lifted, and blessed coolness from Canada flow in, most people greeted it as a second Armistice Day, a time to climb out of their bunkers and celebrate.

Traffic jams clogged roads everywhere, and Highway 50 became a parking lot from Washington to Ocean City. The euphoria ran so high people didn't seem to mind at all. They got out of their cars and vans, set up their lawn chairs on the median, threw frisbees back and forth, and ate picnic lunches. One enterprising caravan of college students even found enough room between their cars to play a screwy sort of volleyball in the middle of the Chesapeake Bay Bridge!

But some people find happiness in places other than the beach. Places like book stores, used book stores—Pandora's Bookstore.

Oh, it feels so great to have a cool day again! mused Jennifer as she drove out onto Highway 50 with the top down for the first time in—well, it *seemed* a year. It felt good to just let her hair fly loose in the wind. As Annapolis loomed ahead of her, she veered off on Riva Road, and then headed south on Highway 2. Stick-um'd to her checkbook were Amy's directions.

"Oh Jen, you'll just *love* it," her closest friend had raved. "It's unlike any other bookstore you've ever seen!"

Jennifer, a veteran of hundreds of used bookstores, strongly doubted that, but not wanting to flatly contradict her friend, she merely mumbled a muffled, "Oh?"

Amy, noting the doubt written on her face (Jennifer never *had* been able to keep a secret for her expressive face gave it away every time) merely grinned and looked wise: "Jus' you wyte, 'enry 'iggens, jus' you wyte!" she caroled.

In the months following that challenge, several other friends had rhapsodized about this one-of-a-kind bookstore, each report torquing up her curiosity another notch. Now, on this absolutely perfect late May day, she saw no reason to delay further: she would see this hyped-way-beyond-its-worth place for herself. After all, there were no other claims on her day. *More's the pity,* she told herself. And her truant memory wafted her backwards (without even asking permission)—backwards to a time when she *had* been needed, *had* been wanted, *had* been loved. *Or,* she qualified to herself, *at least I* thought *he loved me!*

It had been one of those childhood romances adults so often chuckle about. The proverbial boy next door. They had played together day by day, inside one of their homes in bad weather; outside the rest of the time. When school started, they entered first grade together.

He carried her books, fought anyone who mistreated her, and at home they studied together. He'd been the first boy to hold her hand, the first she had kissed. Their parents had merely laughed in that condescending way adults have about young love, and prophesied: "Puppy love *never* lasts. . . . Just watch! They'll each find someone else."

But they didn't find "somebody else." Not even when puberty messed them up inside, re-contoured their bodies, re-directed their thoughts. Each remained the other's all.

They even chose the same college—and studied together still. They went to concerts and art galleries together, hiked the mountains together, walked the beaches barefoot together, haunted bookstores together, went to parties together, and even attended church together.

So it had come as no surprise that spring break of their senior year, when walking among the dunes near Cape Hatteras, he asked her to marry him. And there was no hesitation in her joyous, "Yes, Bill."

That it somehow lacked passion, that there was little yearning for the other physically, didn't seem to matter. Hadn't their relationship stood the test of time? How much longer than twenty years would it take to *know*, for goodness sake!

So the date had been set, the wedding party chosen, the bridal and attendants' dresses made, the flowers ordered, the tuxes measured, the minister and chapel secured, the honeymoon destination booked, the apartment they would live in arranged for, the wedding invitations sent out.

And then—36 hours before the wedding—her world had caved in on her. He had come over and asked if they could talk.

"Of course!" she had smiled, chalking up the tense look on his face to groom-jitters.

They sat down in their favorite swing on the back porch, and looked out at the yard, already festive for the reception to be held there. Her smile faded quickly as she took in his haggard face, his eyes with dark circles around them. Premonition froze her into glacial immobility. Surely it couldn't be what she, deep down, sensed it would be. Not after all these years!

But it was. He could only stammer brokenly the chopped up words and phrases that would amputate two dreams that over a twenty-year period had grown within hours of becoming one. He had found someone whose presence—or absence— raised him to the skies or plunged him to the depths, someone who ignited his hormones to such an extent that life without her was unthinkable. Bill hadn't gone far before his face turned scarlet and he began to sputter.

In mercy, Jennifer broke in: "Don't say anything more, Bill," she cried in a strangely ragged voice. "You can't force love—not the real lifetime kind. I . . . I'd far rather know this now than later. . . ." She paused for control.

Bill could only sit there miserably, his head in his hands.

So it was up to her to finish this thing. She knew she would always love him; after all, he had been her best friend for almost as far back as she could remember. And there is no trap door to open and dump such things—for the memories remain always and cannot be so easily disposed of.

He couldn't bring himself to face her parents, so after a few more minutes they stood up, there was one last hug—and he walked away.

She salvaged a bit of her battered pride by calling off the wedding herself. That was the hardest thing she had ever done. Numbly, she phoned them all, but gave no reasons. They would know why soon enough, if they didn't know already.

And so her marital dreams had died.

A year passed, and another, and another, until six years separated her from that fateful parting that, like "no man's land," separated the girl from the woman. On one side, trust and unconditional acceptance; on the other, suspicion and reserve.

During that first two years, she turned down all the men who asked her out. But, gradually, as her bludgeoned self-esteem began to get up off the floor, she belatedly realized that life must go on, that she must not wall herself off from living. So she began to date again, but not very often. Nine months of the year the children in her third-grade classroom were her world. During the other three she took graduate work, traveled, wrote, visited art galleries, attended plays, concerts, and operas. Often alone, but frequently with dear friends such as Amy, or with her brother James.

She sometimes wondered if she'd ever find the kind of mate Bill had found: the kind of magnetism that would call her even across the proverbial "crowded room." Would there ever be someone who would set her heart singing? Who would be the friend Bill had been, but who would also arouse a passionate yearning to be his physical, mental, social, and spiritual mate? Every once in a while, she would wonder, *Why is it so difficult to find the one? Is there something wrong with me?*

So the long hours, days, weeks, months, and years passed. She completed her Masters at Johns Hopkins, and she was invariably doing something, anything, to avoid admitting to herself that she was unutterably lonely.

None of her diversions worked.

Not one.

Oh, she'd almost missed her road! She slammed on the brakes, almost getting rear-ended in the process, and turned left. "Three and seven-tenths miles," Amy had said. Sure enough, there loomed the sign: PANDORA'S BOOKS.

Gotta be a story here somewhere, she smiled. Now she slowed and turned into an ancient-looking brick gateway. Just inside another sign announced that this was a wildlife sanctuary. *Some bookstore!*

The road snaked its way through first-growth trees (according to report, one of the only such stands of timber left on the Chesapeake). Here and there azalea, rhododendrum, and wild laurel bushes banked the road.

She slowed the Camaro to a crawl, to give some deer time to get off the road. Birds seemed to be everywhere—cardinals, goldfinch, sparrows, even a couple of bluebirds—and high overhead, hawks and gulls. It seemed incongruous, this close to the Washington metroplex of six million people, to discover such solitude.

At last the road straightened out and dropped down into the strangest parking lot she'd ever seen. Following directions from a sign, she drove into another grove of trees, finally finding a pull-in without a vehicle in it. After putting the top up and locking the car, she found a path to the beach.

She sensed the water's edge before she could see it, and now she could plainly hear the *ca-ca-ca-ca*-ing of the gulls. Suddenly, there it was: blinding white clapboard, framed by the silver-flecked blue of the Chesapeake. No clouds overhead today, only seagulls; and on the water, like swans taking flight, sailboats, as far as the eye could see. She stopped, transfixed, and inwardly spoke these words to her best Friend.

Lord, thank you for this day—this almost-too-beautiful-to-be-true day.

She had always been more intense than any of her friends, more deeply affected by beauty.

Before going in, she added a rather strange postscript: *Lord, please let only good things happen to me today.* Then she opened the door and walked in.

Inside, classical music was playing softly, meshing wondrously with the lapping of the waves on the shore, the *ca-ca-ca-ca*-ing of the gulls, and the occasional raucous croak that could come only from the long throat of a great blue heron.

And ah, that one-of-a-kind fragrance of old books, which to book-lovers is the true wine of life! And not marred, as is sadly true of so many used book stores, with disorganization, overstocking, clutter, and grime. But this was blessedly different. She set out to analyze it and find out why.

First of all, it was clean. Not antiseptically so—but just close enough. No grime besmirched the shelves, books, walls, windows, or the floor. Second, although the store contained tens of thousands of books, there was no perception of clutter or of being engulfed by the sheer mass of it all. Why that was so was easy to see: masses of books were broken up by old prints, paintings, sculpture, bric-a-brac, and flowers. *Real* flowers. She could tell that by their fragrance! And the windows— today, *open* windows—to let in the outside world. Or just enough of it. And there were benches and soft chairs everywhere, graced by lamps of great beauty.

Quickly, she discovered that the art work tied in perfectly with the genre displayed on the shelves. For instance, Remingtons and Russells dominated the walls of the western room, supplemented by dust jacket originals, magazine art, movie posters, lobby cards, and old photographs. The adolescent/youth section had as its focal center a wondrous display of Maxfield Parrish, with its pièce-de-résistance, the largest print she'd ever seen of his *Ecstasy*. Blow-ups of dust-jackets, paperbacks, and magazine art graced the walls in just the right places.

And amazingly, different music played in every room. Softly. In the western room could be heard most of the old standard western artists, from The Sons of the Pioneers to Eddy Arnold. In the religion and philosophy room, she heard the great music of the church. Lilting happy music, children, love flowed from the children's room.

But best of all was the literature and general fiction room. For one thing, it dominated the seaward side of the second story. And on walls where no direct sunlight would fade what hung there, she saw faithfully reproduced copies of old masters: Zurburan, Titian, Leonardo, Ribera, Caravaggio, De la Tour, and Rembrandt. A massive stone fireplace anchored the southeastern corner. Just to its right stood a nine-foot grand piano. On its shiny surface was flopped in abandoned comfort as beautiful a Himalayan as Jennifer had ever seen. Without even thinking, she crossed the room towards it and reached out her hand, allowing it to be sniffed before she ventured to scratch the cat's head and massage its ears. A loud purring told her that she had been accepted into the narrow circle that could induce purring.

Jennifer crossed to one of the open windows, leaned against the sill, and gazed out across the silver-flecked blue water. Then, (ever so softly, floating out of the very walls it seemed) she heard those haunting first bars of Chopin's Étude in E. . . . It was just too much: her intensely passionate nature could handle only so much circuit overload. She lost all track of time or reality.

Coming up the stairs with a load of books for re-stocking, Arthur sighed. On this seemingly perfect day he longed to be outside. But so did his employees, so he had let many of them go. Reluctantly. As he heard Étude in E, he slowed his pace.

No matter how often he heard it, that Étude got him every time. Something in its melody brought an ache, reminded him that he was alone—incomplete. Thus his normal defenses melted like wax when he stepped into the room which housed his classics—and stopped, rooted to the floor, when he saw the figure staring out the window. Her sapphire blue dress draped long, loose, and Maxfield Parrish classical; her complexion cameo ivory; her long hair a copperish flame, her ankles and Teva-sandaled feet slim and graceful. A pre-Raphaelite painting suddenly come to life there in the room. He hardly dared breathe lest he break her trance.

Subconsciously, he weighed the external pieces that added up to the totality. No, he concluded, *she is not beautiful, though she has classical features and classical form, but she's alive, as alive as any woman I've ever seen.* He watched, as the strains of Étude in E internalized in her heart and soul and overflowed into her face (that face that always mirrored her inner self in spite of all efforts to control it). A tear glistened in her eye, the color of which he could not see from that angle, and slowly made a pathway down her cheek. But in her reverie she did not even notice it. Strangely enough, even though he'd never seen her before, he yearned to wipe that tear away and find out what caused it—if it was the Étude . . . or if it was something more.

Something woke her, told her she was no longer alone. She turned slightly and saw him standing there, photographing her with his blue-gray eyes. (Hers, he now discovered, were an amazingly burnished emerald green). Gradually, as the mists of her reverie dissipated, he came into full focus. He stood 6'2", dark brown hair salted with premature gray; trim, physically fit. Dressed well, in a button-up chambray shirt, khaki dockers, and slip-on loafers. In his mid-to-late thirties, she guessed.

But his face . . . , she felt instinctively that this man standing there knew pain, for it etched his face. Especially did she note it in the ever-so-slight droop of a mouth that seemed made for smiling. His eyes, she concluded, were wonderfully kind. (He was not photographing her with pin-up intentions, but with tenderness and concern; and for such ammunition, she had no defense. Until that moment, she had never needed any.)

Feeling a familiar softness rubbing against his leg, he looked down and smiled. She liked that smile, and wished to prolong its stay. Clearing her throat, she spoke just one word, "Yours?"

And his smile grew broader as he tenderly picked up the purring cat, cradled it in his muscular arms, and announced, "Pandora."

She laughed, a delightfully throaty laugh, and retorted, "So here's the *real* owner of all these books!"

He laughed too. "Yes, well it's a long story. . . . If you're not in a hurry, I'll tell you."

I'm not in a hurry, she decided. *Never in less of one—in all my life.*

So they sat down on opposite ends of a sofa, and he told her the saga of a Himalayan kitten who got into *everything*! (hence her name), and how she had wrapped her tiny little soul around his when things weren't going very well for him (Jennifer sensed that admittance to be a major understatement). So when certain developments made possible this bookstore, in gratitude, he had named it in her honor.

And he smiled again. "It is her bookstore. . . . I'm sure she feels it is hers, perhaps more so than a human ever could. And our customers, well, the people who come here feel she is boss. Everyone asks about her, and no one ever wants to leave without paying his or her respects." He chuckled again, "I'm not so important; not many feel short-changed if they leave without seeing me."

She thought, but did not say, *I'm afraid—I'm very afraid . . . that I would.*

So interested did she become in the story of this wonderfully different bookstore that she kept at him until the entire story spilled out. Even—or perhaps *especially*—a brief account of the motivation for it: the failure of a relationship central in his life. He did not elaborate.

Other book-lovers came and went, eyed the man, woman, and dozing cat on the couch, attempted to listen in, then reluctantly moved on. Three times, they suffered interruptions: once for a customer downstairs, once for a phone call, and once by refreshments brought up by the assistant manager. Noticing Jennifer's raised eyebrows, he explained that fresh-brewed coffee (straight and decaf) and herbal tea was always ready on both floors, as were bagels and cookies, cold sodas, and bottles of fruit juice.

"Yeah," he admitted, "coffee's one of my besetting sins . . . the jump-start that gets me going. Maybe it isn't very smart to mix coffee and snacks with books, but, real book lovers rarely mistreat books. No one's wrecked a book yet because of it! But no smoking! I can't stand it, and—" he looked down at the sleeping cat on his lap—"neither can Pandora."

Suddenly, Jennifer looked at her watch and jumped to her feet: "I can't believe it. Where has the day gone? So sorry, but I gotta' run. Thanks ever so much for everything, but I'm late for an appointment. But I'll be back! Bye-bye, Pandora." She stopped to give the cat one last scratch under the chin, then she was gone, without so much as revealing her name. But then, Arthur mused, *neither did I!*

With her departure, although there remained not a cloud in the sky, a partial eclipse darkened the sun. To Arthur the day had lost its brightness. The droop came back to his lip, but not—not quite so pronounced as before.

Jennifer stayed away for almost two weeks, but each day she felt the magnetic pull; then she'd recoil from her inner yearning to return: *How silly! How ridiculous to blow out of proportion a simple little conversation. He'd probably talk like that to anyone who came by and asked the same questions. After all, he's in the business to make customers and sell books!*

Finally, thoroughly confused by her inner turbulence, she went back—and he wasn't there! But books are books, and she soon lost herself among them. She wanted to ask about him but could find no reason that didn't seem transparently obvious. However, she did find the books in the vicinity of the check-out stands to be unusually interesting. She kept taking them off the shelves, one at a time, studying them intently, then returning them to the shelves, all without remembering anything about them! She blushed crimson when it suddenly came to her what she was doing. Scolding herself, *You foolish, foolish schoolgirl, you!* she sheepishly put the last book back on the shelf and moved towards the next room.

She had not waited in vain, however. While she was passing the first cash register, she heard someone ask the clerk where the boss was. She slowed her pace. The clerk's voice was low and pleasing to listen to: "Mr. Bond?"

"Yes, of course! Mr. Bond!"

"Oh, . . . uh, . . . he didn't tell me where he was going . . ."

Jennifer's sharp ears then picked up a whispered jab from the clerk at the next register: "But you surely wish he had, huh?"

Jennifer sneaked a look. The face of the first speaker flamed scarlet, her blush speaking volumes. *So that's the way the wind blows!* she thought. She appraised the girl carefully: (young, at most mid-20's); statuesque, with midnight black hair (undoubtedly Hispanic), and strikingly beautiful. . . .

Even more confused than when she came in, Jennifer hurried out of the bookstore without even looking up Pandora. She was disturbed, angry, and more than a little jealous of this girl who got to work there all the time.

The three-digit heat returned after the Memorial Day reprieve, and the steamy humidity slowed life to a gasping crawl. Since it was patently too hot to do other than wilt like an unwatered impatien outside, Jennifer returned again to Pandora's Books.

Looking for him, but not looking for him, she reconnoitered her way through the various rooms, restless as a child the last afternoon of school.

Suddenly, she saw him, sitting on an easy chair by the empty fireplace, a portable phone at his ear. And curled around the back of his neck like a fur stole (and just as limp) was Pandora.

Her eyes twinkling, she surreptitiously edged her way out of the room, assuming he'd not seen her. Eventually, she gravitated back to the children's room, in the center of which was a sunken playground; and apparently, there were *always* children playing there. . . . After browsing awhile, she found a book she had always wanted to read, but could never find: Alcott's *Flower Fables*; sinking into a soft chair with a seraphic sigh of pure joy, she opened its covers.

But she was not to sink into another world so easily. Across from her, a sandy-haired little boy of about five was vainly trying to capture his mother's attention: "Mama, Mama . . . please, Mama, will you. . . ."

"Oh don't bother me!" she snapped.

Undeterred, the little boy persisted: "But Mama, I found this pretty book, and uh . . . I wonder if you'd . . ."

"Oh, for goodness sake! Will you leave me alone!" she snarled.

At this, the boy recoiled, as if struck, and lips quivering, backed away. After one last look at the unyielding face of his mother, engrossed in an Agatha Christie thriller, he turned and headed towards a raven-haired woman who was restocking books across the room. But his courage wavered as he approached the clerk. Would she rebuff him, too?

By now, Jennifer had forgotten her book completely: *How will the Spanish beauty respond to a child's need?* she asked herself. She didn't have to wait long to find out for the woman, on being tapped on the leg by little fingers, whirled around in surprise—but she did not smile. She'd been enduring a raging migraine that afternoon. Milliseconds later, her dark eyes scanned the room to see if anyone had seen. Satisfied that no one had—Jennifer was watching her through veiled eyes (a trick women have and men do not)—she brusquely turned her back to the child, and continued restocking the shelf.

The little boy didn't cry. He didn't say anything at all. He merely turned around, and just stood there, the book still in his hand, lips trembling, and a tear finding its way down his cheek.

It was just too much! Mother or no mother, clerk or no clerk, Jennifer swiftly left her seat and swooped down like a protective hen; then slowed, knelt down, and spoke words kind and gentle, "Can *I* help, dear?" And she tenderly wiped away the tear.

But he had been hurt that afternoon—hurt terribly!—and was no longer as trusting as he'd been only minutes before. He just looked at her, eyes still puddling. She, respecting his space and his self-hood, didn't touch him again—only waited, with tenderness in her eyes. It was no contest. An instant later, vanquished by those soft eyes, he was in her arms, his eyes wet, his little shoulders heaving, but making not a sound.

Across the room, his mother continued reading.

When the little body had stopped shaking, and the tears had ceased to flow, Jennifer led him to a near-by couch, sat down, and drew him to her. Then she asked him about the book. As he slowly turned the pages, and read some of the words, she helped him with the others, and explained the illustrations. A look of joy transfigured his face, and excited comprehension filled his voice . . . if one had been there to see it. . . .

Arthur, who *had* entered the room just in time to catch the entire tableau—*had* seen it. But Jennifer did not see *him*, neither then nor when she took the boy across the room to find another book, his hand held trustingly in hers.

Withdrawing quietly from the scene, Arthur returned to his office, asked his secretary to field all his calls and inquiries, and shut the door. He walked over to the window and looked unseeingly out on the iron-gray bay.

The next time, she came on a rainy afternoon. Evidently a lot of other people agreed with her that a bookstore was the best place to be on such a day. Long lines piled up behind the cash registers, and many people waited with questions. The clerks, she noticed, tried to be helpful, and answered all questions politely and with the obvious willingness to go the second mile. They knew many customers by name.

Even the Hispanic girl. From time to time, Jennifer saw the girl turn to see if a certain gentleman remained in his office. Then, when Mr. Bond finally *did* come out, the girl's cheeks flamed as she looked everywhere but in his direction. A number of people clustered around him, asking questions, and each one received that same warm smile and attitude of eager helpfulness.

Then the Hispanic girl went up to her boss to ask a question. Jennifer didn't fail to notice both the smile he gave his lovely clerk and the rapt expression in the girl's eyes. *Hmm.*

She moved on to the American writers section, looking for some of her favorite authors. *Oh! What a selection of Harold Bell Wright! I've never seen this many in one place before!* She took down a dust-jacketed *Exit.* No sooner had she done so than she felt a presence behind her.

"Are you into Wright?" a familiar voice asked.

She turned, smiled (*I like her dimples,* Arthur observed to himself), and said, "Well, sort of. I've read five or six, but I've never seen this one—or, for that matter, a number of the others here. Rarely do I see more than a few of his books in any one place."

"Well, there's a reason for that . . . uh . . . Miss—it *is* Miss . . . ?"

"Yes," and she found his steady gaze, kindly though it was, more than a bit disconcerting; "my last name is O'Riley."

"Mine," he grinned a little wickedly, is Bond. But not"—(obviously he had used this line many times before, she concluded)—"James . . . but Arthur."

"And I answer to Jennifer," she said, blushing.

Ignoring the opening, he returned to Wright, "Well, Miss O'Riley, Wright books are hard to get, and harder to keep in stock. . . . Might I ask which ones you've read?"

"Well, the first of his books I read when I was only seventeen. Read it one beautiful day on California's Feather River Canyon. I was visiting a favorite aunt and uncle at the time—will never forget it, for it changed my life."

"I'd guess it was one of his Social Gospel Trilogy," he broke in.

"Trilogy?" she asked. "There's a trilogy?" The one I read was *The Calling of Dan Matthews,* and it really changed my life."

"Oh?" he asked quizzically.

She stumbled a bit for words, finally stammering out, "I just don't know how to go on . . . and I don't know yet if . . . if . . . uh . . . "

"If I'm a Christian?" he finished for her.

"Yes."

"Well, I am. Why do you ask?"

"Oh, it's just that *The Calling of Dan Matthews* gave me a new vision of God, of His all-inclusiveness. I'm afraid I had been rather elitist before I read that book."

He laughed (*conspiratorially*, she thought), "I agree, Miss O'Riley. It hit me that way, too. Only, I had read *That Printer of Udell's* first—by the way, it anchors the Trilogy—so I was somewhat prepared for his contention that Christ's entire earthly ministry was not about doctrine at all . . . but about—"

"Service," she broke in softly.

"Yes, service for others," he agreed.

They talked a long time about Wright that day, and after that about other authors of mutual interest as well. Some, they loved in common; others they did their best to convert the other to.

Arthur had always felt he could more than hold his own in any battle of wits, but he discovered that in Jennifer, he had met his match. One day, as they sparred back and forth on the historical romances of Rafael Sabatini (while each had favorites, both agreed on the one that stood out above all others, *Scaramouche,* that great tale of the French Revolution), he winced—*she never misses a trick . . . not a nuance escapes her!*

Not long after, during another visit, she found a copy of a book she'd searched for, for years: Gene Stratton Porter's *The Fire Bird*. She quickly found a quiet niche, settled down in an easy chair, turned up the lamp, and began leafing through the book. She held no illusions about buying it, though. Beautiful and rare, true—but the price was far too high for *her* budget.

Then she heard voices, one of which sounded very familiar. She pulled in her feet so as to be as inconspicuous as possible. When the voices drew nearer, she drew her legs under her, yoga style. Since the speakers sat down in the alcove just before hers, she couldn't help but overhear:

"I just don't know what I'm going to do, Mr. Bond!" quivered a woman's voice: "I really don't. Lately . . . I . . . I . . . just feel even the good Lord has forsaken me."

"*That*, Mrs. Henry, I can assure you is not true. The Lord *never* forsakes His children," he responded.

"Oh, but Mr. Bond, you just don't know! Or you wouldn't be so sure. My oldest son—you remember Chris! . . . Well, he's on drugs. Worse than that: he's become a pusher . . ." Her voice broke. "And Dana—I . . . I . . . I just found out she's pregnant. I just can't believe it. She grew up so faithful at attending church every week. . . . And the man, the man who . . . uh . . . uh . . ."

"The father of the unborn baby?"

"Yes. He attends our church, too."

"Oh. Are they planning to marry?"

"That's the worst part. He says it's all her fault for not taking precautions. Won't have anything more to do with her. And Dana's near desperate. I'm afraid she'll, she'll—" And again her voice broke.

Arthur's voice broke in, firmly and kindly. "Mrs. Henry, there's no time to lose. Is Dana home this afternoon?"

Answered in the affirmative, Arthur led Mrs. Henry out, and after explaining to the clerks that an emergency had come up, he and Mrs. Henry hurried through the heavy rain to their cars.

For a long time Jennifer just sat there, thinking. *Just what kind of bookstore—what kind of man—was this?*

Jennifer came back within the week, and shamelessly stayed within listening range of where he worked. She simply *had* to know, for sure, what manner of man this was. So many times before, she'd been disappointed, disillusioned—so why should this one prove to be any different?

She was, by turns, amazed, then moved, by what she overheard. Apparently, he possessed endless patience, for she never heard him lose his temper, no matter what the provocation. Even with bores, who insisted on talking on and on about themselves. She discovered that while most asked book-related questions, a surprisingly large number of these people felt overwhelmed by life and its problems. In Arthur, they found, perhaps not always solutions, but at least a listening, sympathetic ear. In used bookstores, she had discovered, there appears to be an implied assumption: one finds an ear, no matter how stupid, inane, or ridiculous the topic may be. In that respect, used bookstores function as courts of last resort: the last chance to be heard before outright despair sets in. But, in Arthur's case, it went far far beyond mere listening—for he genuinely *cared!*

At last came August, and with it pre-session. Vacation was over, for school would begin in a few weeks. So busy was she that it was almost Labor Day before she got back to Pandora's Books. Just as she was leaving, he came out of his office and smiled at her. On the confidence of that smile, she walked over to him and asked if he could spare a moment.

"Of *course*!" he replied, and steered her into a quieter room, then seated her by an open window. The heat had finally broken, and the cool bay breeze felt like heaven.

During the small talk that followed, she became increasingly aware of how strongly she was affected by this man, this tangible synthesis of strength, wisdom, and kindness. She was more aware of being near him than she had ever been with any other man. Stumbling a bit over her words, she asked him if he ever spoke to students about books—not just singly but in the schoolroom itself.

"Often, Miss O'Riley."

For some unaccountable reason, she blushed.

Pandora chose this moment to demand attention, and he lifted her up into his arms, where she ecstatically began to purr and knead her claws into him.

"You see, Miss O'Riley," he continued, "they represent our future. There can be no higher priority than children."

She found herself inviting him to speak to her class, and he gladly accepted.

As she drove home, and her Camaro left a trail of greenish-yellow leaves dancing in her wake, she acknowledged to herself that she'd just, by that act, set forces in motion—forces that might breach almost any wall she'd built up through the years.

Apprehensive she was, a little. But she sang an old love song over and over all the way home—not realizing until her garage door opened on command, just what she'd been singing.

He *came*! And the children loved him! He came with a big box of books and sat down on the floor with them, holding them enthralled by stories that came from those books . . . and the men and women who illustrated them. And he answered each of the many questions they asked. The ones he couldn't, he promised to answer the day their teacher brought them on a field trip to his wildlife sanctuary/book store, when they could meet Pandora.

Jennifer pulled back from her usual focal center to give him the opportunity to be in control. She needn't have bothered. She knew now that when he walked into a room, it was as if he was iridescent, for he attracted all eyes just as if he shone like the sun. Just as was true—though she didn't know it—of herself.

She watched his every move, listened to his every word, and watched the quicksilver moods as they cavorted on his face and danced in his blue-gray eyes—eyes with the impishness of the eternal child in them. Like the legendary Pied Piper of Hamlin, he so enthralled that the children would have followed him *anywhere*.

And he, though apparently he saw nothing but the children, never missed a nuance of her. The vision she made, leaning against the window, would hang in the galleries of his mind for all time: a Dante Gabriel Rossetti dream woman. Her long bronze hair, ignited by the late morning sun, her emerald green dress, and her seize-the-day face, added up to far more than mere beauty.

Before he left, he let each child choose a favorite book—and left the rest for the room library. Then, after reminding them to come see Pandora soon, he was gone . . . and the halcyon day clouded over. But the sun came back out again when one curious little boy sneaked to the window and caught sight of Mr. Bond getting into his '57 Thunderbird. His awestruck "Wow!" brought the entire class to the window in seconds, and they all waved—and he, catching the motion at the window, waved back as the coral sand-colored convertible sped out of sight.

But not out of memory.

But just to make sure, that afternoon a florist delivered a large autumn floral display, crowned by a couple of book-topped spears, and at the very top, a goldish-brown cat.

That night, he called. Did she want to go with him to the Kennedy Center to hear the Vienna Boys' Choir? *Is the Pope Catholic?*

Not long after, his second call came, asking her to attend church service with him. After that, the telephone worked both ways. Concerts, the many galleries and exhibits of the Smithsonian, opera; rides to the seashore, to quaint restaurants in old inns; and hikes along mountain trails—all these brought roses to her cheeks and a glow into her eyes.

After Thanksgiving dinner at her folks, he told her to bundle up for a rather chilly ride. Always, it seemed with him, the top stayed firmly down—he reveled in the panoramic view. On and on the Bird sped, and as she nestled down, the excitement brimming over in her eyes and the way her sapphire blue paisley scarf set off her flaming mane of hair—well, it made it mighty difficult to keep his eyes on the road.

The population thinned out as the Bird's deep throat rumbled into old St. Mary's City.

Here, they stopped by the river for a while, ostensibly to watch the geese, but in reality, because he felt reflective.

"You know, Jennifer, I think it's time I told you a little more about my failed marriage."

"That's up to you, Arthur."

"Let's see, how do I start? . . . Well, I had known Marilyn for a number of years; we attended the same parochial high school, same college—even same church. . . . My folks were good friends with her folks—had been for many years. . . . We liked the same things, shared many of the same dreams."

She listened, gazing out at the river.

"Actually," Arthur laughed, a strangely undefinable laugh, "I don't think I ever actually proposed—we just drifted into it. All our friends, our families, our folks, took it for granted. So we married. We loved each other. *That*, I'm sure of. It was to be for life—at least it was for me."

There was a long pause, as he searched for the right words.

"We were married about 18 months. Then, one never-to-be-forgotten spring morning, after breakfast, she announced that marriage was 'a bore,' 'a drag,' and that she wanted to regain her freedom."

A pause, then in a flat voice, he continued. "So she divorced me, and found another—several anothers. That was about twelve years ago, but it seems like yesterday. . . . Oh, I floundered for a time; my self-esteem was at its all-time low." Then he brightened: "But God saw me through. I escaped to the New England coast—stayed there a long time, healing. It was there that the epiphany came to me: Pandora's Books."

"Oh!" she breathed, half a sigh, half a paean.

"Yes, a dream bookstore—unlike any I had ever seen or heard about. . . . But the Lord showed me that mere business success would not be enough: I must also care for His sheep. *That* would be my ministry. And the frosting on the cake. . . ."

"Was Pandora," Jennifer finished.

"Yes, Pandora," he smiled as he started the engine, and again they were out on the highway, heading south.

I'm so glad he told me! she murmured to herself as the Bird gathered speed. *He didn't walk out on her! That's what I was afraid of. . . . He had to have been hurt more than I was, yet he didn't let it destroy him. There was closure—a long time ago. . . And joyously, there's a clear road ahead! Oh Lord, thank you!* And her heart began to sing.

Then she lost all track of time as the Bird raced down the peninsula, churning up waves of gold, brown, orange, crimson, and green leaves in its wake. Suddenly, there ahead was only a narrow strip of land, banked by white-capped water, slate-blue below and white-winged gulls in cloudy sky above. The Bird nosed into a parking space at the end of the road: Route 5, dead-end. Since it was both cold and blustery, they had it all to themselves.

For a few minutes they just sat there, watching and listening to the gulls. She wondered what he was thinking.

Leaning back, his hands behind his head, he finally broke into her reverie: "You know, Jennifer, this is what I miss most. Solitude. The solitude you can still find out west and up north. So many people live here that, after a while, one gets claustrophobic. At least I do. If anything ever moves me away from this bay, it will be that. Well, that and my beloved mountains. I miss them."

Suddenly, he shifted in his seat and laughed. "Am I ever the gabby one today! Enough about me. What about *you*? What is *your* story? Hasn't some armor-clad knight tried to gallop away with you?"

Shyly, she answered, "Y-e-e-s."

Well, what happened?" he demanded, an impish look in his eyes. "'Fess up: I did my stint, now it's your turn."

So she told him . . . and took a while doing it.

When she finally finished, he sat in silence a while, then smiled, "I'm glad. Someday I may tell you why."

"Someday you may, huh," she laughed, her eyes narrowing.

"You know, Jennifer, your voice has bells in it . . . your laugh, most of all. Even on the phone, I hear bells ringing when you speak. You radiate happiness."

She blushed, started to say something, then stopped.

"Go on," he chuckled. "Might as well get it out."

"Oh!" she said, trying to slow her racing heart. "It's just that I've been happy a lot lately . . . and . . . and"—refusing to meet his eyes—"*you're* to blame."

There! It was out, and her eyes fell, unable to meet his.

Silence thundered in her ears, and when at last she looked up, he was looking out to sea, with an enigmatic look on his face. His body had tensed, his face was now rigid. She felt utterly humiliated by her admission.

Then he turned, placed his hand on hers butterfly-briefly, and said, "Well, it's getting late. What do you say to heading back?"

All the way back, she wallowed in misery: *Why did I wreck what had been so perfect? Why change gears when we were just beginning to gain momentum in the lower one?*

Once she caught him eyeing her pensively.

When he walked her to her door, they didn't banter as usual. He didn't ask her for another date, just said in a flat voice, "Thank you, Jennifer, for a perfect Thanksgiving!"

That was a long *long* night for Jennifer. To herself, she wailed, *Stupid me! I've blown it! I took a wonderful friendship, just beginning to bud, and wrecked it. Might just as well have demanded the full-blown rose! But that's just it: I'm in love with him. Been in*

love with him for a long time—just refused to admit it. He storms me in his quiet, gentle way. I . . . I . . . I've never met anyone before who lights up every room he's in—at least for me. I know it's shameless: but here am I—in my 30's—having never known passion (wondering if I even had it in me!), and now, with this man, I yearn for him, long for him, desire him, with every inch of my body, heart, and soul!

Her thoughts raced on. *Friendship alone is no longer enough—even if, as is all too obvious!—it is to him. My passionate heart cries for far more. I cannot be merely another in a long line of friendships—perhaps even romances—with him.*

If only, if only, though, I had waited, perhaps it would have come.

Oh why, oh Lord, did I do it! Oh God . . . to find my soul's other half—after all these long years—and then to lose him because of my big big mouth!

And she wept, through that endless night.

When he called, as usual, to ask her to attend church with him, she turned him down in an icy voice, then cut the conversation short by saying, "I'm sorry . . . but gotta run—I'm late!" and hung up. Then she was miserable, for in reality she had nothing else to do at all, and an entire evening to mope about it.

Jennifer had always loved the Christmas season, a time when being a child again became an accepted thing. With what joy she always greeted the wreathes and garlands, the multicolored lights on the neighborhood eaves and trees, the Advent candles, the Christmas trees seen through the windows, the Christmas carols played continuously by radio stations! This year, though, she just wished it would go away. Even in her schoolroom. True, she decorated it in the usual way, drilled the children for the big Christmas program, and helped them make personalized gifts for those dearest to them. But it all seemed hollow, all a sham. Even God, she felt, irrationally, had somehow let her down: *Lord, how could You do this to me? How could You let me make such a fool of myself!*

She no longer kidded herself about what Arthur meant to her. Or that he could be but a passing fancy that would go away. No, for better or for worse, he'd be a deep-rooted part of her as long as she lived.

He did not call again. Several times—nay, a hundred times!—she felt the urge to call him and apologize for her curtness on the phone, but her lacerated pride just would not let her.

Her last papers had been corrected and the scores added up, gifts had been accepted from each of her students, and the big program—to which she'd once planned to invite Arthur—had gone off without a hitch . . . yet none of it meant anything to her. Nothing at all.

Finally, it was over for another fall.

On a certain dismal winter evening, she was sitting there in her undecorated townhouse, wallowing in misery and self pity, wishing for him, *yearning* for him, and dreading Christmas week.

The phone rang.

She answered it, but no bells rang in her voice, just a subdued "hello!" Almost she hung up when she heard his voice on the other end, inwardly raging because his voice still possessed this power over her, giving her goose bumps. It just didn't seem fair! But there was something different in his voice, almost a pleading note. He had a big favor to ask of her, he said.

"A favor?" she snapped, and then could have choked her misbehaving other self for that snippiness.

Silence swirled around her. Then he continued, more haltingly this time. He had a big favor to ask, yes, but with a qualifier or two thrown in. First of all, he wanted her to share *The Messiah* with him at Washington's National Cathedral, and secondly, he wanted to show her something of extreme importance.

When the silence on the other end of the line continued, he gulped and added, "If you'll accept just this once, I'll promise not to ever bother you again."

Seeing no graceful way out of it, she grudgingly parted with an undernour-ished "yes."

There! Finished! That will end it. No ellipsis, no dash, no exclamation mark. Period! Period! Period! . . . But three periods would be an open-ended ellipsis! shouted an irrational thought from a far corner of her brain.

Her mind raced, her thoughts milling in chaotic confusion: *I shouldn't have said yes, that I'd go . . . but I'd hate to miss out on going! I don't think I can handle being close to him again—I'm so sure my face will give me away if my big mouth doesn't. Yet how can I possibly give up this one last time—the last time we'll ever be together? Oh, it will tear my heart out to be close to him and not be able to touch him! Not to be able . . . Oh! Oh! Yet I don't want him to take anyone else there! Certainly—make that double certainly!—not that Hispanic beauty! Oh! What am I gonna wear?*

The big evening (the last evening! she promised herself) finally came. She dressed carefully in her favorite blue gown, a Diane Fries she'd purchased, in a rare fit of recklessness, from Nordstrom. She'd make it a swan song to remember. Then she put on her heavy black cashmere coat, bought on sale just before I. Magnin closed.

The doorbell rang, her pulse quickened. She forced herself to walk very slowly to the door, lest she appear too eager. *Oh, I'm a despicable vixen!* she reprimanded her misbehaving other self.

When she opened it and saw him standing there, in spite of her well-planned intentions, sapphire stars sparkled in her eyes and her cheeks crimsoned. For he was so . . . so . . . so detestably dear.

At the curb, its motor purring, was a car she'd not seen before, a Mercedes 560, in a color a suspiciously emerald sort of green.

"Wouldn't dare park the Bird in D.C." was his only explanation as he helped her in.

Outside the window, the white of the first snowfall of the year enveloped the world. Christmas CDs played softly through the sophisticated sound system, and she relaxed a little in spite of herself.

Neither one said much during the ride to the cathedral.

They had a tough time finding a parking space, but finally did, then joined the well-dressed throng filling the streets. Excitement flooded Jennifer's cheeks, and once or twice she trembled as Arthur's hand brushed hers.

Inside the world's sixth largest cathedral, all was Christmas, and Arthur moved, with Jennifer just behind him, toward the nave. He took her hand now to keep her close. Eventually they arrived at the spot where he felt the acoustics to be nearly perfect, and they found a pillar on which to lean, for the seats were all taken.

Then the organ found its voice, shaking the near-century-in-the-making building, and chills went up her spine. Pipe organs had that power over her. She sneaked a sideways glance at him and felt satisfied by the look of awe on his face. Then the orchestra, then the soloists, then the choirs, and then she lost all track of time as Handel transported her through the drama of the ages.

Through it all, she remained aware of him, but in a sort of haze. He left once and brought back two chairs. She sank down with a sigh of relief. After a couple of hours, unconsciously declaring a temporary truce, she took advantage of his tall frame next to her and leaned her head against him. She felt him tremble when a draft of cold air blew a strand of her flame-colored hair across his face.

Soaring upward, her soul drank deeply of the majesty of the mighty columns, and graceful arches that portrayed the architectural yearning for the Eternal. The words and music and organ and choirs and soloists and cathedral battered her sensibilities into a pulp. It was too much of a sensory overload for mere flesh and blood. During the "Hallelujah Chorus," when she stood at his side, she again felt him tremble, and peeped sideways to find him wiping away tears. Since she was crying too, she felt a renewed sense of kinship with him.

The crowd was unbelievably quiet as they found their way out, almost as if words seemed far too fragile to accommodate such divine freight.

On the slippery road again, neither spoke, and the sound system remained silent, as if anything else right now would be anticlimactic. For this she inwardly thanked him, for his sensitivity and empathy. For not shattering the mood.

So surreal was it all that she didn't even notice they had passed her highway exit until the Mercedes veered off Highway 50 onto Riva Road. To her raised eyebrows, he merely smiled and said, "Remember, there's more yet to this promised evening."

As the traffic thinned out south of Annapolis, and the flocked evergreens flashed by, slowly, haltingly, he began to speak.

"Undoubtedly . . . you . . . you . . . uh wondered about my strange response to your—uh—to what you said about yourself . . . the last time we were together."

She stiffened: *How dare he bring up that utterly humiliating afternoon, when he rejected my stupid disclosure of my inner feelings. How* dare *he!*

But he ploughed on, not looking at her. "You see, Jen,"—he'd never called her by her family pet name before!—I was so wounded, so scarred, by the rejection I told you about . . . that I determined that never again," and here he struggled for control, then continued—"never again would I let a woman get that close to me."

He paused, and she hardly dared breathe.

"But it's been hard, Jen, because I'm still young . . . and lonely. It's been very hard."

Inadvertently, her lesser self got in another lick: "The beautiful black-haired girl who works for you?"

He almost hit a tree, but when he turned toward her, his face had relaxed just a little: "How did you know?"

"I have eyes. Any woman could have told you."

There was a long silence as he searched for the right words. Finally, as if he'd given up finding any better ones, the refrain again: "It's been hard." But he did not tell her that it was the Hispanic beauty's lack of tenderness, her repulsing of the little crying boy, that had turned the tide of his life.

Neither did he tell her about the effect *she* had made on him that same day: a Raphael madonna, tenderly holding a child.

After a time, he continued. "You see, Jen, I could not take such rejection twice in one lifetime. I'm afraid it would . . . uh . . . destroy me!" He paused again. "Marriage for me is for life—even if our society seems to disagree with me." Here, his words seemed sadly bitter to the wondering woman at his side. "And marriage without God to cement it is dead-end! I don't see how any marriage can last a lifetime without a Higher Power to anchor it. All around me, I see marriage after marriage, live-in relationships galore, collapse, so few making it through. I have been afraid. I'm not ashamed to admit it, Jen: I've been terribly afraid to even consider marriage again!"

She remained silent. Numb.

"As for children, and what divorce or separation does to them . . . . There are simply no words in the dictionary terrible enough to fully describe what it does to them, to their feelings of self-worth. I see it every day. And I don't yet know what to do, what to say, to their anguish—anguish so intense it's long since wrung out all the tears they can cry."

And she, remembering those lonely, deep-scarred wounded ones in her classes, could only nod her head.

"And then you came," he added, groping for the right words. You scared me.

He caught her whispered "Scared?"

"Yes. . . . Scared. For you were, well, what I never had, yet had always wanted. In a way, too good to be true. Jen, I never expected to find such a woman as you. So, when you told me last Thanksgiving that I . . . that I made you happy, like an absolute fool, I panicked! I had blocked such a future out of the realm of the possible for so many years that when it came, I just . . just didn't know how—"

Suddenly, he slowed and turned down a familiar road, now a fairyland in snow. Her heart began to thud so loudly she felt certain he must overhear it. Then he turned down a road she'd never noticed before, and made a long wide turn.

Suddenly, directly ahead, in a blaze of holiday lights, stood Pandora's Books. It was so beautiful that her lips formed an O, and her hands flew to her face. She didn't see his relieved smile.

Inside, festive music played in every room, only all the same track this time. Christmas decorations were everywhere, as were lights and trees of various sizes.

"I've always loved Christmas—kinda never grew up," he said simply.

Unconsciously, she groped for his hand.

He showed her each room, and her delighted response and the restored bells in her voice, were all he could have hoped for. Finally they came back to the office area and he stepped briefly behind the counter, where he must have flicked a switch, for suddenly silence shattered the mood, and she was alone with him in the big building.

He walked back to her, and she raised her emerald eyes to his, seeking to find something that had not been there before. Suddenly she heard music again—froze for a moment—and whispered, "Étude in E."

"Yes."

"Why, Arthur? I don't understand what you're trying to—"

Softly placing his finger on her lips, he whispered, "Listen!"

She listened. And, as she knew it would—it always had—it melted her. And, as she knew she would—she always had—she cried.

Fire blazed through her tears, and she accused, "How could you! You *know* how that étude affects me. I saw you watching me that day."

Know? Yes, he knew. *She's right. It's come. . . . It's all come down to this question, this moment,* he thought. *I hurt her terribly by my inexcusable fear of commitment. . . . And now I must answer. But one thing is certain: this is no time for half-hearted measures. Words . . . words can be such inadequate things! How can I make her know?*

Gathering her in his arms, he answered softly, "I just *had* to, dear . . . dearest."

Her wounded pride struggled to assert itself. *How dare he assume I'd forgive him this easily for the hell he put me through—how dare he!*

In the end, her pride lost. Gentle, he remained, but as immovable as Gibraltar. The Étude was on his side too—it was two against one. She felt her resistance ebbing. Then she made the mistake of trying to read the expression on his face—not easy, considering the dim light in the room. But what she saw there closed forever all avenues of escape. It was love. Love undiluted, unqualified, undistilled, unreserved, undivided—he had cleared the deck of his heart of everything else but *her*.

Her struggles ceased, and all the lights of the world came on in her eyes as her arms stole up and closed behind his neck. Then it was, as the shackles of fear and regret fell clanging to the floor, that he started to tell her in mere words how much he loved her, but she, cutting his words off with her lips, showed him a better way. A far better way.

Some time later, Arthur sensed a familiar presence at his ankles. Looking down, but not releasing Jennifer from the prison of his arms by so much as one link, he smiled and said, "Sorry Pandora, you jealous ol' thing. From now on, you're just gonna' have to *share*!"

ACKNOWLEDGMENTS

"Love at Christmas" (Introduction) by Joseph Leininger Wheeler. Copyright © 2008. Printed by permission of the author.

"The Littlest Orphan and the Christ Baby," by Margaret E. Sangster, Jr. Included in Sangster's anthology, *The Littlest Orphan and Other Christmas Stories* (New York: Round Table Press, 1928). If anyone can provide knowledge of earliest publication source of this old story, please send to Joe Wheeler (P.O. Box 1246, Conifer, CO 80433).

"The Yule Miracle," by Albert Payson Terhune. Reprinted by permission of Girl Scouts of the USA.

"Under the Banana Leaf Christmas Tree," by Carolyn Rathbun-Sutton. Reprinted by permission of the author.

"A Love Song for Christmas," by David T. Doig. Published in December 1987 *Good Housekeeping*. Reprinted by permission of Rosalind Doig.

"Christmas Lost and Found," by Shirley Barksdale. *McCall's, Reader's Digest,* and *Chicken Soup for the Soul* have carried this story. Reprinted by permission of the author.

"The Good Things in Life," by Arthur Gordon. Included in Gordon's anthology, *Through Many Windows* (Old Tappan, New Jersey: Fleming H. Revell, 1983). Reprinted by permission of Pamela Gordon.

"O Little Flock," by Temple Bailey. If anyone can provide knowledge of earliest publication source of this old story, or the whereabouts of the author's next of kin, please send to Joe Wheeler (P.O. Box 1246, Conifer, CO 80433).

"Good Will Toward Men," by Harry Harrison Kroll. Published in December 23, 1933, *Young People's Weekly*. Text printed by permission of Joe Wheeler (P.O. Box 1246, Conifer, CO 80433) and David C. Cook, Colorado Springs, CO).

"The House that Glowed," by Arthur S. Maxwell. Published in Volume 7 of *Uncle Arthur's Bedtime Stories* (Hagerstown, Maryland: Review and Herald Publishing, 1964). Reprinted by permission of Audrey Maxwell Zinke and Review and Herald Publishing, Hagerstown, MD.

"Bobo and the Christmas Spirit," by Edith Ballinger Price. If anyone can provide knowledge of first publication source and author's next of kin, please send to Joe Wheeler (P.O. Box 1246, Conifer, CO 80433).

"The Real Christmas Spirit," by Helen E. Richards. Published in December 25, 1923, *The Youth's Instructor*. Reprinted by permission of Joe Wheeler (P.O. Box 1246, Conifer, CO 80433) and Review and Herald Publishing, Hagerstown, Maryland.

"A Tree for Benji," by Harold Ivan Smith. Reprinted by permission from *Charisma & Christian Life*, December 1951. Copyright © Strang Communications Co., USA. All rights reserved.

"The Red Envelope," by Nancy N. Rue. Published in December 1997 *Focus on the Family Magazine*. Reprinted by permission of the author.

"And You Shall Receive," by Louis Arthur Cunningham. Published in December 1945 *Canadian Home Journal*. Reprinted by permission of the relatives of the late Mrs. Hortense Cunningham.

"A Stolen Christmas," by Charles M. Sheldon. Published in *Fifty Years of Christmas* (New York: Rinehart & Company, 1951). Reprinted by permission of Christian Herald, Inc.

"Guest in the House," by Helen Marie Amenaude. Reprinted by permission of Christian Herald, Inc.

"Eric's Gift," by Deborah Smoot. Published in December 1989 *Plus Magazine*. Reprinted by permission of the author.

"Pandora's Books," by Joseph Leininger Wheeler. First published in *Christmas in My Heart 6* (Hagerstown, MD: Review and Herald Publishing, 1997). © 1997. Reprinted by permission of the author.